PENGUIN CLASSICS
Maigret Travels

'Extraordinary masterpieces of the twentieth century'
– John Banville

'A brilliant writer'
– India Knight

'Intense atmosphere and resonant detail . . . make Simenon's fiction remarkably like life'
– Julian Barnes

'A truly wonderful writer . . . marvellously readable – lucid, simple, absolutely in tune with the world he creates'
– Muriel Spark

'Few writers have ever conveyed with such a sure touch, the bleakness of human life'
– A. N. Wilson

'Compelling, remorseless, brilliant'
– John Gray

'A writer of genius, one whose simplicity of language creates indelible images that the florid stylists of our own day can only dream of'
– *Daily Mail*

'The mysteries of the human personality are revealed in all their disconcerting complexity'
– Anita Brookner

'One of the greatest writers of our time'
– *The Sunday Times*

'I love reading Simenon. He makes me think of Chekhov'
– William Faulkner

'One of the great psychological novelists of this century'
– *Independent*

'The greatest of all, the most genuine novelist we have had in literature'
– André Gide

'Simenon ought to be spoken of in the same breath as Camus, Beckett and Kafka'
– *Independent on Sunday*

ABOUT THE AUTHOR

Georges Simenon was born on 12 February 1903 in Liège, Belgium, and died in 1989 in Lausanne, Switzerland, where he had lived for the latter part of his life. Between 1931 and 1972 he published seventy-five novels and twenty-eight short stories featuring Inspector Maigret.

Simenon always resisted identifying himself with his famous literary character, but acknowledged that they shared an important characteristic:

> My motto, to the extent that I have one, has been noted often enough, and I've always conformed to it. It's the one I've given to old Maigret, who resembles me in certain points . . . 'understand and judge not'.

Penguin is publishing the entire series of Maigret novels.

GEORGES SIMENON

Maigret Travels

Translated by HOWARD CURTIS

PENGUIN BOOKS

PENGUIN CLASSICS

UK | USA | Canada | Ireland | Australia
India | New Zealand | South Africa

Penguin Books is part of the Penguin Random House group of companies
whose addresses can be found at global.penguinrandomhouse.com

Penguin
Random House
UK

First published in French as *Maigret voyage* by Presses de la Cité 1957
This translation first published 2018
002

Set in 12.5/15 pt Dante MT Std
Typeset by Jouve (UK), Milton Keynes
Printed in Great Britain by Clays Ltd, St Ives plc

ISBN: 978-0-241-30382-5

www.greenpenguin.co.uk

Maigret Travels

15 Sept., 2018

Is this the same
story as "Maigret
Travels South"
listed in my ORIGINAL
"BOOK LISTS" which
I noted as an
"OMNIBUS"?

Recall: FOR some
REASON, I had
listed "Mag. and
the Saturday
Caller" as an
"OMNIBUS" and
it was NOT!
DUH!!

1.

What happened at the George-V while it was raining in Paris, Maigret was sleeping and a certain number of people were doing their best

'The most troublesome cases are those that seem so commonplace at first that you don't attach any importance to them. They're a bit like those illnesses that start in a subdued way, with a vague sense of unease. By the time you finally take them seriously, it's often too late.'

This was something Maigret had said to Inspector Janvier as they crossed Pont-Neuf on their way back to police headquarters on Quai des Orfèvres one evening.

But tonight, Maigret made no comment on the events currently unfolding, because he was fast asleep beside Madame Maigret in his apartment on Boulevard Richard-Lenoir.

If he had been anticipating trouble, he certainly wouldn't have thought of the Hôtel George-V, a place more often talked about in the society pages of newspapers than in the local news, but of a deputy's daughter he had been obliged to summon to his office and advise to refrain from further bad behaviour. Although he had spoken to her in a fatherly tone, she had taken it quite badly. True, she had only just turned eighteen.

'You're nothing but a civil servant, I'll see to it that your career is ruined . . .'

By three in the morning, a fine drizzle was falling, which although barely visible still lacquered the streets and gave a sheen to the lights, like tears to eyes.

At 3.30, on the third floor of the George-V, a bell rang in the room where a chambermaid and a valet were dozing. They both opened their eyes, but the valet was the first to notice that the yellow light had come on.

'It's for Jules,' he said.

That meant that someone had rung for the waiter, who set off to take a bottle of Danish beer to a customer.

The two servants dropped off to sleep again on their respective chairs. There was a relatively long silence, then the bell rang again just as Jules, who was over sixty and had always done the night shift, returned with his empty tray.

'Here goes!' he muttered between his teeth.

Unhurriedly, he headed for suite 332, where a light was on above the door, knocked, waited a moment and, hearing nothing, gently opened. There was nobody in the dark sitting room. A little light came from the bedroom, where a faint, continuous moaning, like that of an animal or a child, could be heard.

The little countess was lying on the bed, her eyes half closed, her lips slightly parted, both hands on her chest more or less where the heart was.

'Who is it?' she moaned.

'The waiter, countess.'

He knew her well. She knew him well, too.

'I'm dying, Jules. I don't want to. Call the doctor, quickly. Is there one in the hotel?'

'Not at this hour, countess, but I'll tell the nurse.'

Just over an hour earlier, he had brought a bottle of champagne, a bottle of whisky, some soda and an ice bucket to this same suite. The bottles and glasses were still in the sitting room, apart from one champagne glass that lay on the bedside table, tipped on its side.

'Hello? Get me the nurse, quickly!'

Unsurprised, Mademoiselle Rosay, the duty operator, inserted a plug in one of the switchboard's many sockets, then another.

Jules heard a distant ringing, then a sleepy voice.

'Hello, infirmary here.'

'Could you come down right away to suite 332?'

'I'm dying, Jules . . .'

'You're not going to die, countess.'

He wasn't sure what to do while waiting. Switching on the lamps in the sitting room, he noticed that the bottle of champagne was empty, whereas a quarter of the bottle of whisky was still untouched.

Countess Palmieri was still moaning, her hands taut on her chest.

'Jules . . .'

'Yes, countess?'

'If they come too late . . .'

'Mademoiselle Genévrier is on her way down now.'

'But if they come too late, tell them I poisoned myself, but that I don't want to die . . .'

The grey-haired, grey-faced nurse, whose body, beneath

her white coat, still smelled of bed, entered the suite after tapping at the door for form's sake. She was holding a brownish bottle of something or other in her hand, and her pockets were stuffed with boxes of pills.

'She says she poisoned herself.'

Before anything else, Mademoiselle Genévrier looked around her, spotted the waste-paper basket, took a tube from it and read the label.

'Ask the switchboard operator to call Dr Frère. Say it's urgent.'

Now that there was someone to take care of her, it was as if the countess were abandoning herself to her fate, making no further attempt to speak, her moaning growing fainter.

'Hello? Call Dr Frère quickly. No, not me, the nurse is asking for him.'

Such things are so frequent, in luxury hotels and in some parts of Paris, that when the police emergency switchboard receives a call at night from the sixteenth arrondissement, for example, there is almost always someone who asks:

'Barbiturates?'

It has become a generic name for this kind of suicide attempt.

'Fetch me some hot water.'

'Boiling?'

'It doesn't really matter, as long as it's hot.'

Mademoiselle Genévrier had taken the countess's pulse and lifted her eyelid.

'How many pills did you take?'

'I don't know . . .' she replied in a little girl's voice. 'I can't remember . . . Don't let me die . . .'

'Of course not, my dear. Just drink this.'

An arm round her shoulders, she held a glass in front of her lips.

'Is it bad?'

'Drink.'

Not far away, on Avenue Marceau, Dr Frère hastily dressed and grabbed his bag. Soon afterwards, he left the sleeping building and got into his car, which was parked outside.

The marble lobby of the George-V was deserted apart from the night receptionist reading a newspaper behind his mahogany desk on one side and the porter doing nothing on the other.

'Suite 332,' the doctor said as he passed.

'I know.'

The switchboard operator had told him all about it.

'Shall I call an ambulance?'

'Let me see first.'

Dr Frère knew most of the hotel's suites. Like the nurse, he knocked more or less symbolically, then went in, took off his hat and headed straight for the bedroom.

After fetching a jug of hot water, Jules had withdrawn to a corner.

'She took something, doctor. I gave her . . .'

They exchanged a few words, which were like shorthand or like a conversation in code, while the countess, still supported by the nurse, retched violently and began to vomit.

'Jules!'

'Yes, doctor.'

'Put a call through to the American Hospital in Neuilly and ask them to send an ambulance.'

There was nothing exceptional about any of this. The switchboard operator, headphones on her head, spoke to another night-shift operator over in Neuilly.

'I don't know for sure. It's Countess Palmieri. The doctor's upstairs with her now.'

The telephone rang in 332. Jules picked up the receiver.

'The ambulance will be here in ten minutes,' he announced.

Having just administered an injection, the doctor put the syringe back in his case.

'Shall I dress her?'

'Just wrap her in a blanket. If you see a suitcase anywhere, pack a few of her things. You know better than I do what she'll ask for.'

A quarter of an hour later, two male nurses took the little countess downstairs and put her in the ambulance, while Dr Frère got back in his car.

'I'll get there the same time as you . . .'

He knew the nurses. The nurses knew him. He also knew the hospital's switchboard operator, with whom he had a few words, as well as the young doctor on duty. These people, too, spoke little and in a kind of code, used as they were to working together.

'Room 41 is free.'

'How many pills?'

'She can't remember. The tube was found empty.'

'Has she vomited?'

This nurse was as familiar to Dr Frère as the one at the George-V. As she got down to work, he at last lit a cigarette.

Pumping of the stomach. Taking of the pulse. Another injection.

'All we can do now is let her sleep. Take her pulse every half hour.'

'Yes, doctor.'

He went back down in a lift just like the one in the hotel and gave some instructions to the receptionist, who wrote them down.

'Have you informed the police?'

'Not yet.'

He looked at the black and white clock. 4.30.

'Put me through to the police station in Rue de Berri.'

There were bicycles outside the door of the station, under the lamp. Inside, two young officers were playing cards, and a sergeant was making coffee on a spirit lamp.

'Hello, Rue de Berri station . . . Dr What? . . . Frère? . . . All right, go ahead . . . Just a moment . . .'

The sergeant grabbed a pencil and noted down what he was being told on a scrap of paper.

'Yes . . . Yes . . . I'll tell them you'll be sending your report . . . Is she dead?'

He hung up and said to the other two, who had been watching him:

'Barbiturates. George-V . . .'

As far as he was concerned, it was just one more chore. With a sigh, he picked up the receiver again.

'Central switchboard? . . . Rue de Berri station here . . . Is that you, Marchal? How are things over there? . . . Pretty quiet here . . . The fight? . . . No, we didn't keep them. One of them has a lot of contacts, if you know what I mean. I had to phone the chief inspector, and he told me to let them go.'

The fight he was referring to had taken place in a night-club in Rue de Ponthieu.

'Anyway, I have something else. Barbiturates. Are you taking this down? . . . Countess . . . Yes, a countess . . . Whether she's a real one or not, I have no idea . . . Palmieri . . . P for Paul, A for Arthur, L for Léon, M for . . . Palmieri, yes . . . Hôtel George-V . . . Suite 332 . . . Dr Frère . . . American Hospital in Neuilly . . . Yes, she did say something. She wanted to die, and then she changed her mind. The usual story . . .'

At 5.30, Inspector Justin of the eighth arrondissement questioned the night porter of the George-V, made a few notes, then spoke to Jules, the waiter, after which he headed for the hospital in Neuilly, where he was told that the countess was asleep and that her life was no longer in danger.

At eight in the morning, it was still drizzling, but the sky was clear. Lucas, who had a slight cold, took his seat behind his desk at Quai des Orfèvres, ready to look through the night's reports.

Here, couched in bureaucratic language, was mention of the fight in Rue de Ponthieu, a dozen prostitutes arrested, a few drunks, a knife attack in Rue de Flandre and a few other incidents, none of them out of the ordinary.

Six lines also informed him of the suicide attempt by Countess Palmieri, née La Salle.

Maigret arrived at nine, somewhat anxious about the deputy's daughter.

'Has the chief asked for me?'

'Not yet.'

'Anything important in the reports?'

Lucas hesitated for a moment, came to the conclusion that an attempted suicide, even one at the George-V, was of no great importance and replied:

'No, nothing.'

He had no inkling that in doing so he was making a serious mistake, one that would cause complications for Maigret and the whole of the Police Judiciaire.

When the bell rang in the corridor, Maigret left his office, carrying a few files, and, along with the other department heads, made his way to the commissioner's office. Here, the cases currently being handled by the various chief inspectors were discussed, but since he knew nothing about her, Maigret did not mention Countess Palmieri.

By ten, he was back in his office. His pipe in his mouth, he began his report on an armed robbery that had occurred three days earlier, the perpetrators of which he was hoping to arrest very soon thanks to an Alpine beret left at the scene.

At about the same time, a man named John T. Arnold, having his breakfast in pyjamas and dressing gown in his room at the Hôtel Scribe, on the Grands Boulevards, picked up the telephone.

'Hello, mademoiselle. Could you please get me Colonel Ward at the Hôtel George-V?'

'Right away, Monsieur Arnold.'

Monsieur Arnold was a long-standing guest who lived at the Scribe virtually all year.

The switchboard operators at the Scribe and the George-V knew each other, as operators do, even though they had never met.

'Morning, dear, can you get me Colonel Ward?'

'Is it for Arnold?'

The two men were in the habit of calling each other several times a day, and the ten a.m. telephone call was a tradition.

'He hasn't rung for his breakfast yet. Shall I call him anyway?'

'Wait. I'll ask my man.'

The plug passed from one socket to another.

'Monsieur Arnold? . . . The colonel hasn't rung for his breakfast yet. Shall I get them to wake him?'

'Has he left a message?'

'They didn't tell me anything.'

'It is ten o'clock, isn't it?'

'Ten past ten.'

'Call him.'

The plug again.

'Ring him, dear. Too bad if he grumbles . . .'

Silence on the line. The switchboard operator at the Scribe had time to put through three other calls, including one from Amsterdam.

'Are you still there, dear? Don't forget my colonel.'

'I keep ringing him. He doesn't answer.'

A few moments later, the Scribe called the George-V.

'Listen, dear. I told my man the colonel isn't answering. He says it's not possible, the colonel is expecting his ten o'clock call, apparently it's very important.'

'I'll ring him again . . .'

Then, after another vain attempt:

'Wait a minute. I'll ask the porter if he's gone out.'

A silence.

'No, his key isn't in the rack. What do you want me to do?'

In his suite, John T. Arnold was getting impatient.

'Well, mademoiselle? Have you forgotten my call?'

'No, Monsieur Arnold. The colonel isn't answering. The porter hasn't seen him go out, and his key isn't in the rack.'

'Let them send the waiter to knock at his door.'

It wasn't Jules this time, but an Italian named Gino, who had taken over on the third floor, where Colonel Ward's suite was located five doors down from Countess Palmieri's.

The waiter called the porter back.

'There's no answer, and the door's locked.'

The porter turned to his assistant.

'Go and have a look.'

The assistant now also knocked, saying in a low voice:

'Colonel Ward?'

Then he took a skeleton key from his pocket and opened the door.

In the suite, the shutters were closed, and a lamp was still lit on a table in the sitting room. The lights were also on in the bedroom, the bed made up for the night, the pyjamas laid out.

'Colonel Ward?'

There were dark clothes on a chair, socks on the carpet, and a pair of shoes, one of them upside down, showing the heel.

'Colonel Ward!'

The bathroom door was ajar. The porter's assistant first knocked, then opened the door and simply said:

'Monsieur!'

He almost telephoned from the room, but was so reluctant to stay there that he preferred to leave the suite, closing the door behind him. Neglecting the lift, he ran down the stairs.

Three or four guests were standing around the porter, who was looking through a transatlantic plane schedule for them. His assistant whispered in his ear:

'He's dead.'

'One moment . . .' Then, only now grasping the words he had just heard: 'What do you mean?'

'Dead . . . In his bath . . .'

The porter asked the guests, in English, to wait a minute. He crossed the lobby and leaned across the reception desk.

'Is Monsieur Gilles in his office?'

The receptionist nodded. The porter went and knocked at a door in the left-hand corner.

'Excuse me, Monsieur Gilles. I just had René go up to the colonel's suite. Apparently, he's dead in his bath . . .'

Monsieur Gilles was wearing striped trousers and a black cheviot jacket. He turned to his secretary.

'Call Dr Frère immediately. He must be busy doing his rounds. See if he can be reached . . .'

Monsieur Gilles knew things of which the police were as yet unaware. So did the porter, Monsieur Albert.

'What do you think, Albert?'

'The same as you, I guess.'

'You heard about the countess?'

A nod of the head sufficed.

'I'm going up.'

But, as he had no desire to go alone, he chose one of the young men in morning coat and slicked-back hair from reception to accompany him. Passing the porter, who had resumed his usual place, he said to him:

'Ask the nurse to come down to 347 immediately.'

The lobby was not empty, as it had been during the night. The three Americans were still discussing which plane to take. A couple who had just arrived were filling in their form at reception. The florist was at her post, as were the newspaper seller and the employee who handled theatre tickets. A few people sat waiting in armchairs, among them the senior sales assistant from a well-known dress shop with a box full of dresses.

Upstairs, standing by the bathroom door in suite 347, the manager did not dare look at the colonel's obese body, which lay curiously in the bath, the head underwater, only the belly emerging.

'Get me the—'

He changed his mind when he heard the telephone ringing in the next room. He rushed to it.

'Monsieur Gilles?'

15

It was the switchboard operator's voice.

'I reached Dr Frère as he was visiting a patient in Rue François-Premier. He'll be here in a few minutes.'

'Who am I supposed to be calling?' the young man from reception asked.

The police, obviously. There was no getting away from them in situations like this. But although Monsieur Gilles knew the local chief inspector, the two men didn't get on well. Plus, the local police sometimes behaved with a tactlessness that ill suited a hotel like the George-V.

'Get me the Police Judiciaire.'

'Who shall I ask for?'

'The commissioner.'

They had met several times at dinners, and although they had only exchanged a few words, that was enough of an introduction.

'Hello? Is that the commissioner? . . . I'm sorry to disturb you, Monsieur Benoit. Gilles here, manager of the George-V. Something has just . . . I mean, I've just discovered . . .'

He no longer knew how to come out with it.

'Unfortunately, this is a very important figure we're talking about, someone known around the world . . . Colonel Ward . . . That's right, David Ward . . . a member of my staff just found him dead in his bath . . . No, that's all I know. I thought it best to call you immediately . . . I'm expecting the doctor any moment now . . . I don't need to tell you that this requires . . .'

Discretion, of course. He had no desire to see reporters and photographers besieging the hotel.

'No . . . No, of course not. I promise we won't touch a thing. I'll stay in the suite in person . . . Ah, here's Dr Frère. Would you like to speak to him?'

The doctor, who as yet knew nothing, took the receiver that was held out to him.

'Dr Frère speaking . . . Yes . . . I was with a patient and have only just arrived . . . What's that? . . . I can't say he's a patient of mine, but I know him . . . I did once treat him for a mild bout of flu . . . What? Oh, no, very robust, in spite of the life he leads – led, I should say . . . I'm sorry, I haven't yet seen the body . . . Of course . . . Yes . . . Yes . . . I understand . . . Good day, commissioner . . . Would you like to speak to him again? . . . No?'

He hung up.

'Where is he?'

'In the bath.'

'The commissioner asks that nothing be touched until he's sent someone.'

Monsieur Gilles turned to the young receptionist.

'You can go down now. Keep an eye open for the people from the police and make sure they come up discreetly. And no chatting about this in the lobby, please . . . Have you got that?'

'Yes, monsieur.'

The telephone rang in Maigret's office.

'Could you come and see me for a moment?'

It was the third time Maigret had been disturbed since he had started his report on the armed robbery. He relit the pipe he had let go out, walked down the corridor and knocked at the commissioner's door.

'Come in, Maigret. Sit down.'

Rays of sunlight were starting to mingle with the rain, and there were some on the commissioner's brass ashtray.

'Do you know Colonel Ward?'

'I've read his name in the papers. He's the one who's been married three or four times, isn't he?'

'He's just been found dead in his bath at the George-V.'

Absorbed as he was by the case of the armed robbery, Maigret did not react.

'I think it best if you go there yourself. The doctor, who's more or less attached to the hotel, has just told me that the colonel was still in excellent health yesterday and that as far as he knows he never suffered from heart problems . . . The press are bound to get hold of it, not just the French press, the foreign papers, too.'

Maigret hated these cases involving well-known people, cases that needed to be handled with kid gloves.

'I'm on my way,' he said.

Once again, his report would have to wait. Grouchily, he opened the door to the inspectors' room, wondering who to take with him. Janvier was there, but he, too, was busy with the armed robbery.

'Go to my office and try to carry on with my report . . . Lapointe!'

Young Lapointe looked up, clearly pleased.

'Get your hat. You're coming with me.'

Then, to Lucas:

'If anyone asks for me, I'll be at the George-V.'

'Is it about the attempted suicide?'

Having blurted it out without thinking, Lucas turned red.

'What attempted suicide?'

'The countess . . .' Lucas stammered.

'What are you talking about?'

'There was something in this morning's reports about a countess with an Italian name who tried to kill herself at George-V. The only reason I didn't tell you—'

'Where's the report?'

Lucas searched through the papers heaped on his desk and pulled out an official sheet.

'She isn't dead. That's why . . .'

Maigret skimmed through a few lines.

'Has anyone questioned her?'

'I don't know. Someone from the eighth arrondissement went to the hospital in Neuilly. I don't yet know if she's in a fit state to speak.'

What Maigret didn't know was that, the previous night, just before two in the morning, Countess Palmieri and Colonel David Ward had got out of a taxi outside the George-V, and the porter hadn't been surprised to see them coming to collect their keys together.

Nor had Jules, the floor waiter, been surprised when, called to the countess's suite, number 332, he had found the colonel there.

'The usual, Jules!' the colonel had said.

That meant a bottle of Krug 1947 and an unopened bottle of Johnny Walker: the colonel didn't trust whisky he hadn't opened himself.

Lucas, who had been expecting a reprimand, was even

more mortified when Maigret looked at him with a surprised air, as if such a lack of judgement, coming from his longest-standing colleague, was impossible to believe.

'Come with me, Lapointe!'

They passed a petty crook Maigret had summoned.

'Come back this afternoon.'

'What time, chief?'

'Whenever you like.'

'Shall I take a car?' Lapointe asked.

They chose a car, and Lapointe took the wheel. At the George-V, the doorman had his instructions.

'Leave it. I'll park it.'

Everyone had instructions. As the two police officers advanced, the door opened, and in the twinkling of an eye they found themselves at the door of suite 347. The manager, informed of their arrival, was waiting for them.

Maigret hadn't often had occasion to work at the George-V, but he had nevertheless been called there two or three times and he knew Monsieur Gilles, whose hand he shook. Doctor Frère was in the sitting room, waiting by the pedestal table, on which he had placed his black instrument case. He was a calm, pleasant man with a long list of patients, a man who knew almost as many secrets as Maigret himself. Only, he moved in a different world, one the police rarely had occasion to enter.

'Dead?'

He nodded.

'About what time?'

'We'll only know for certain after the post-mortem, if, as I assume, a post-mortem is ordered.'

'Couldn't it have been an accident?'

'Come and see . . .'

Maigret was no happier than Monsieur Gilles at the sight of the naked body in the bath.

'I haven't moved him. There was no point, medically speaking. At first sight, it could have been one of those accidents that happen more often in baths than you might think. Someone slips, his head hits the edge . . .'

'I know. Only, that doesn't leave any marks on the shoulders. Is that what you meant?'

Like the doctor, Maigret had noticed two darker patches, similar to bruises, on the dead man's shoulders.

'You think he was helped, is that it?'

'I don't know. I'd rather the pathologist pronounced on that.'

'When did you last see him alive?'

'About a week ago, when I came to give the countess an injection.'

Monsieur Gilles' face clouded over. Had he been hoping to avoid the matter of the countess coming up?

'A countess with an Italian name?'

'Countess Palmieri.'

'The one who tried to commit suicide last night?'

'To be honest, I'm not sure it was a serious attempt. It's true she took barbiturates. In fact, I knew she used them regularly at night. She took a larger than usual dose, but I doubt she ingested enough of them to cause death.'

'A fake suicide, in other words?'

'That's what I'm wondering.'

They were both accustomed to women – almost always

pretty women! – who, after a quarrel, a disappointment, a love affair, take just enough sleeping pills to present the symptoms of poisoning, but without putting their lives in danger.

'You say the colonel was present when you gave the countess an injection?'

'Whenever she was in Paris, I'd give her two a week. Vitamins B and C. It wasn't anything serious. Over-exertion . . . if you know what I mean.'

'And the colonel?'

Monsieur Gilles preferred to answer this question himself.

'The colonel and the countess were very close. They each had their own suite, I always wondered why, because—'

'Was he her lover?'

'It was an open secret, you might almost say it was official. About two years ago, unless I'm mistaken, the colonel asked his wife for a divorce and, in their set, it was expected that once he was free he would marry the countess.'

Maigret almost asked, with false naivety:

'What set is that?'

But what was the point? The telephone rang, and Lapointe looked at his chief to know what to do. It was obvious that he was overawed by the surroundings.

'Answer it.'

'Hello? . . . What? . . . Yes, he's here . . . That's right, it's me.'

'Who is it?' Maigret asked.

'Lucas would like a word.'

'Hello, Lucas.'

To make up for the morning's blunder, Lucas had got in touch with the American Hospital in Neuilly.

'I'm sorry, chief. I'll never forgive myself. Has she come back to the hotel?'

Having been left alone in her room, Countess Palmieri had got up and walked out of the hospital without anyone thinking of stopping her.

2.

In which further reference is made to people who constantly have their names in the papers, although not in the local news

It was about then that the incident happened, something apparently insignificant that was nevertheless to influence Maigret's mood throughout the investigation. Was Lapointe aware of it, or did the chief inspector see a reaction in him that he hadn't had?

Earlier, when Monsieur Gilles had spoken of the set to which Countess Palmieri and Colonel Ward belonged, Maigret had already refrained from asking:

'What set is that?'

If he had done so, wouldn't everyone have sensed a hint of irritation, irony, even aggressiveness in his voice?

He was reminded of an impression he'd had when he was just starting out in the police. He was more or less the same age as Lapointe and had been sent to carry out a simple check in the very same neighbourhood he was in now, between Place de l'Étoile and the Seine – he couldn't remember the name of the street.

Those were still the days of private mansions, and young Maigret had had the sensation that he was entering a new universe. What had struck him most was the quality of the silence, far from the crowds and the din of public transport. The only sounds were the singing of birds and the rhythmical noise of horses' hooves as women and men in light-coloured bowler hats rode by on their way to the Bois de Boulogne.

Even the apartment buildings had an almost secretive look about them. In the courtyards, you saw chauffeurs polishing cars, and sometimes, in a doorway or at a window, a valet in a striped waistcoat or a butler in a white tie.

Of the lives of the masters, almost all of them familiar names you saw in the morning's *Figaro* or *Gaulois*, the inspector, as he then was, knew almost nothing, and there was a tightness in his throat as he rang at those majestic gates.

Of course, today, in suite 347, he was no longer the beginner he had been then. Most of the mansions had disappeared, and many streets that had once been silent had become shopping streets.

Nevertheless, he now found himself in what had replaced the old aristocratic neighbourhoods, and there the George-V stood at the centre of a private world with which he was not especially familiar.

The names of those who were still asleep or having their breakfast in the neighbouring suites were often in the newspapers. Avenue George-V, Rue François-Ier and Avenue Montaigne constituted a world apart where the plates on the buildings bore the names of great fashion houses and where you saw things in the shop windows, even that of a mere shirt-maker, that were unknown anywhere else.

Was Lapointe, who lived in a modest furnished room on the Left Bank, disorientated? Was he feeling, as Maigret had once done, a grudging respect for this luxury he had suddenly discovered?

'A policeman, the ideal policeman, should feel at ease in all kinds of surroundings.'

Maigret himself had said that once, and all his life he had done his best to forget the surface differences between people, to scratch away at the veneer in order to discover the naked human being beneath a variety of appearances.

And yet this morning, despite himself, he was irritated by something in the atmosphere around him. Monsieur Gilles, the manager, was a fine man, in spite of his striped trousers, his professional smoothness and his fear of scandal, as was the doctor, who was used to treating celebrities.

It was rather as if he had sensed a kind of complicity between them. They uttered the same words as everyone else, and yet they were speaking another language. Whenever they said 'the countess' or 'the colonel', it had a meaning that was lost on ordinary mortals.

What it boiled down to was that they were in on the secret. They belonged, even if only in minor roles, to a world apart, a world that Maigret scrupulously insisted on approaching with an open mind.

All these ideas were vague, something he sensed rather than thought as he put down the receiver, turned to the doctor and asked:

'Do you think that if the countess had really swallowed

a dose of barbiturates capable of killing her, it would have been possible, after you had treated her, for her to get up without help half an hour ago and leave the hospital?'

'You mean she's gone?'

The shutters in the bedroom were still lowered, but the ones in the sitting room had been opened, and a little sunlight, more of a reflected glow, was filtering in. The doctor was standing by the pedestal table on which he had put his instrument case. As for the manager of the hotel, he was near the door to the sitting room, and Lapointe to Maigret's right, standing back a little.

The dead man was still in the bath, and the bathroom, the door to which remained open, was the most brightly lit room.

The telephone rang again. The manager picked up the receiver after a glance at Maigret, as if asking his permission.

'Hello? . . . Yes, speaking . . . Is he coming up?'

Everyone was looking at him, and he was searching for something to say, an anxious expression on his face, when the door to the corridor was pushed open.

A man of about fifty, with silvery hair, suntanned, wearing a light grey end-on-end suit, looked from one to another of the figures gathered in the room and at last spotted Monsieur Gilles.

'Ah, there you are! What's happened to David? Where is he?'

'I'm sorry, Monsieur Arnold.'

He pointed towards the bathroom then, quite naturally, started speaking English.

'How did you hear?'

'I phoned five times this morning,' Arnold replied in the same language.

That was another detail that increased Maigret's irritation. He could understand English, with a degree of effort, but was far from fluent in it. Now the doctor, too, took up that language.

'I'm afraid, Mr Arnold, there's no doubt that he's dead.'

The newcomer had moved to the doorway of the bathroom and now stood there for a while looking at the body in the bath. His lips moved as if he were saying a silent prayer.

'A stupid accident, don't you think?'

For some reason, he had reverted to French, which he spoke with hardly any trace of an accent.

It was at that exact moment that the incident took place. Maigret was near the chair on which the dead man's trousers had been thrown. There was a thin platinum chain hanging from a button at the height of the belt, a chain that was probably attached at the other end to an object in the pocket, a key or a watch.

Mechanically, out of pure curiosity, Maigret reached out his hand to grab the chain and, just as he was doing so, the man named Arnold turned and threw him a stern look, as if reprimanding him for inappropriate or tactless behaviour.

It was all much subtler than words. Just a glance, not even especially emphatic, a barely perceptible change of expression.

But Maigret let go of the chain and assumed an attitude of which he was immediately ashamed, because it was the attitude of a guilty man.

Had Lapointe really noticed and had he deliberately turned his head away?

There were three officers at headquarters – it had become a subject for much humour – whose admiration for Maigret verged on worship: Lucas, who had been there the longest, Janvier, who had once been as inexperienced and passionate as Lapointe, and 'young Lapointe' himself, as everyone called him.

Had he been disillusioned, or merely embarrassed, on seeing his chief caught out, as he himself was, by the atmosphere in which they found themselves immersed?

Maigret reacted by turning harsher. He was well aware that that, too, might have been tactless, but he couldn't do otherwise.

'I need to ask you a few questions, Monsieur Arnold.'

The Englishman did not ask him who he was, but turned to Monsieur Gilles, who explained:

'Detective Chief Inspector Maigret, from the Police Judiciaire.'

A vague, barely polite nod.

'May I ask you who you are and why you came here this morning?'

Once again, Arnold looked at the manager in some bewilderment, as if the question was surprising to say the least.

'Monsieur John T. Arnold is—'

'Would you mind letting him answer for himself?'

'Do we think we could move into the sitting room?' the Englishman asked.

Before they did so, he went and took another look at the bathroom, as if once again paying his respects to the dead man.

'Do you still need me?' Dr Frère asked.

'As long as I know where to find you . . .'

'My secretary always knows where I am. And the hotel has my telephone number.'

Arnold said in English to Monsieur Gilles:

'Could you have them bring me up a scotch, please?'

Before resuming the interview, Maigret picked up the telephone.

'Could you get me the prosecutor's office, mademoiselle?'

'What office is that?'

They didn't speak the same language here as at Quai des Orfèvres. He gave the number.

'I'd like to speak to the prosecutor or one of his deputies . . . Detective Chief Inspector Maigret . . . Yes . . .'

While he was waiting, Monsieur Gilles found time to say in a low voice:

'Could you please ask those gentlemen to act with discretion, to come into the hotel as if everything's normal and . . .'

'Hello? . . . I'm at the Hôtel George-V, sir. We've just found a dead body in a bathroom here, Colonel David Ward . . . Ward, yes . . . The body's still in the bath and there are indications that it wasn't an accidental death . . . Yes, so I've been told.'

The prosecutor had just said, at the other end of the line:

'You know that David Ward is a *very important* man?'

Maigret nevertheless continued listening patiently.

'Yes . . . Yes . . . I'll be here . . . Something else happened last night in the same hotel. I'll tell you about it later . . . Yes . . . See you soon, sir.'

While he'd been speaking, a waiter in a white jacket had put in a brief appearance, and Monsieur Arnold had settled into an armchair, slowly and carefully cut the end of a cigar and lit it.

'I asked you—'

'Who I am and what I'm doing here. Let *me* ask *you* a question: do you know who my friend David Ward is – or, as I suppose I must say now, was?'

It might not have been rudeness after all, just an innate self-confidence. Arnold was at home here. The manager was reluctant to interrupt him, and when he finally did so it was rather in the manner of a schoolboy in class asking permission to go to the toilet.

'Please excuse me, gentlemen. I'd like to know if I can go down and give a few instructions.'

'We're still waiting for the prosecutor.'

'Yes, I heard that.'

'We're going to need you. I'm also waiting for the technicians from Criminal Records and the photographers, as well as the pathologist.'

'Could I let at least some of those gentlemen in through the service entrance? I'm sure you understand, inspector. If there are too many comings and goings in the lobby and—'

'I do understand.'

'I'm very grateful . . . Your whisky will be right up, Monsieur Arnold. Will you have something, gentlemen?'

Maigret shook his head and then regretted doing so: he could have done with a stiff drink.

'I'm listening, Monsieur Arnold. You were saying . . . ?'

'I was saying that you've probably seen my friend David's name in the newspapers, like everyone else. Most often, it's preceded with the word billionaire. The "English billionaire". If you count in francs, it's correct. Not in pounds.'

'How old was he?' Maigret cut in.

'Sixty-three . . . David wasn't a self-made man. As we say in England, he was born with a silver spoon in his mouth. His father already owned the biggest wireworks in Manchester, which was founded by his grandfather. Are you following me?'

'Yes.'

'I wouldn't go so far as to say that the business ran itself and that David didn't need to have anything to do with it, but it didn't demand much of him, the occasional conversation with his directors, board meetings, papers to sign . . .'

'He didn't live in Manchester?'

'Almost never.'

'If the newspapers are to be believed . . .'

'The newspapers have permanently adopted two or three dozen celebrities and report the slightest thing they do. That doesn't mean that everything they report is accurate. A lot of inaccurate things have been printed about

David's divorces, for example . . . But that's not what I'm trying to convey to you . . . As far as most people were concerned, David, having inherited a large fortune and a well-established business, had nothing else to do but go gallivanting around Paris, Deauville, Cannes, Lausanne or Rome, frequenting nightclubs and race-courses, surrounded by pretty women and people as well known as he was. But it wasn't so.'

Arnold took his time, gazed for a moment at the white ash of his cigar and signalled to the waiter, who had just come in.

'Do you mind?' he said, taking the glass of whisky from the tray. Then, settling comfortably in his armchair: 'The reason David didn't stay in Manchester and live the usual life of a big English industrialist was precisely because his position there was all mapped out for him and he simply had to continue the work of his father and grandfather, which didn't interest him. Can you understand that?'

From the way he looked at Maigret, then at young Lapointe, it was clear that he considered the two men incapable of understanding such a feeling.

'The Americans have a word we English don't use much. They talk about a "playboy", which means a rich man whose sole aim in life is to have a good time, play polo, practise winter sports, attend regattas, haunt nightclubs in pleasant company—'

'The prosecutor will be here soon,' Maigret said, looking at his watch.

'I'm sorry to inflict this speech on you, but you asked

me a question that can't be answered in just a few words. And perhaps I'd like to save you making any blunders . . . Far from being a "playboy", David Ward was involved in a number of different businesses – involved personally, not as the owner of the Ward Wireworks in Manchester. Only, he didn't think his work required him to shut himself away in an office for eight hours a day. Please believe me when I tell you that he had a brilliant business brain. He could make incredible deals in the most unexpected places and at the most unexpected times.'

'Could you give me an example?'

'One day, we were driving together in his Rolls on the Italian Riviera and had a breakdown that forced us to stop at a fairly modest tavern. As they were making us a meal, David and I went for a walk in the surrounding area. This was twenty years ago. By that evening, we were in Rome, but a few days later, on David's behalf, I bought two thousand hectares of land partly covered in vines. Today, there are three big hotels there, plus a casino and one of the prettiest beaches on the coast, lined with villas . . . In Switzerland, near Montreux—'

'In other words, you were his business associate.'

'His friend and his business associate, if you want to put it that way. His friend first of all. Before I met him, I'd never been involved in anything commercial or financial.'

'Are you also staying at the George-V?'

'No, at the Hôtel Scribe. You may think it strange, but in Paris and elsewhere, we almost always stayed at different hotels. David was very protective of his privacy.'

'Is that the reason Countess Palmieri had a suite at the other end of the corridor?'

Arnold turned slightly red.

'That reason and others . . .'

'Meaning what?'

'It's a delicate matter . . .'

'Wasn't everyone aware of their relationship?'

'Certainly everyone talked about it.'

'And was it true?'

'I suppose so. I never asked any questions.'

'And yet you were close.'

It was Arnold's turn to be irritated. He, too, must be thinking that they didn't speak the same language, that they weren't on the same level.

'How many times was he married?'

'Only three. The papers said it was more than that, because whenever he met a woman and went out with her a few times, they'd say he was getting married again.'

'Are his three wives still alive?'

'Yes.'

'Any children?'

'Two. With his second wife, a son named Bobby, who's sixteen and in Cambridge, and with his third wife, a daughter named Ellen.'

'Was he on good terms with them?'

'With his ex-wives? On excellent terms. He was a gentleman.'

'Did he ever see them?'

'He'd occasionally run into them.'

'Are they wealthy?'

'The first one, Dorothy Payne, is. She belongs to an important textile-manufacturing family in Manchester.'

'What about the other two?'

'He's made sure they're well taken care of.'

'So none of them would benefit from his death?'

Arnold seemed shocked, frowning like a man who doesn't quite understand.

'Of course not!'

'What about Countess Palmieri?'

'He would almost certainly have married her once his divorce from Muriel Halligan became final.'

'Who, in your opinion, would benefit from his death?'

The reply was as rapid as it was unambiguous.

'Nobody.'

'Do you know if he had any enemies?'

'As far as I know, he had only friends.'

'Was he planning to stay at the George-V for much longer?'

'Wait. It's October 7th now . . .'

He took a red notebook from his pocket, a handsome notebook with a soft leather cover and gold corners.

'We got here from Cannes on the 2nd. Before that we were in Biarritz, after leaving Deauville on 17 August . . . We were due to leave on the 13th for Lausanne.'

'On business?'

Once again, Arnold looked at Maigret with a kind of despair, as if this thick-headed man was permanently incapable of understanding the most basic things.

'David has a suite in Lausanne. In fact, that's his official address.'

'And here?'

'He has this suite all year round, too, just as he has one in London and another at the Carlton in Cannes.'

'What about Manchester?'

'He owns the Ward family house, which is a huge Victorian building. I don't think he slept there more than twice in thirty years. He always hated Manchester.'

'Do you know Countess Palmieri well?'

Arnold didn't have time to answer the question. Footsteps and voices were heard from the corridor. Monsieur Gilles, more impressed than he had been by Maigret, led in the prosecutor and a young examining magistrate Maigret hadn't yet worked with. His name was Calas, and he looked like a student.

'Let me introduce Monsieur Arnold—'

'John T. Arnold,' the Englishman said, getting up from his chair.

'The dead man's close friend and business associate,' Maigret said.

As if delighted to finally be dealing with somebody important, perhaps somebody from the same world as him, Arnold said to the prosecutor:

'I had an appointment with David at ten o'clock this morning, or to be more precise, I was due to phone him at that time. That's how I learned of his death. Now I'm told it may not have been an accident, and I assume the police have good reasons for saying that. What I'd like to ask you, monsieur, is to avoid this matter causing too much of a stir. David was an important man, and I can't tell you all the repercussions his death will have, not only on the stock exchange, but in many different circles.'

'We'll be as discreet as possible,' the prosecutor said. 'Isn't that so, inspector?'

Maigret bowed his head.

'I assume,' Arnold went on, 'that you have questions to ask me?'

The prosecutor looked at Maigret, then at the examining magistrate.

'Later, perhaps, I don't know yet. For the moment, I think you can go.'

'If you need me, I'll be downstairs in the bar.'

Once the door had closed behind him, they looked at each other anxiously.

'Nasty business, isn't it?' the prosecutor said. 'Any ideas yet?'

'No, none. Except that a certain Countess Palmieri, who was Ward's mistress and who had a suite at the end of the corridor, tried to kill herself last night. The doctor had her taken to the American Hospital in Neuilly, where she was given a private room. The nurse looked in on her every half hour. Not long ago, she found the room empty.'

'You mean the countess has disappeared?'

Maigret nodded, adding:

'I'm having the railway stations, the airports and the roads out of Paris watched.'

'Curious, don't you think?'

Maigret shrugged. What could he say? Everything in this case was curious, from the dead man, who had been born with a silver spoon in his mouth and who did business while spending time at race-courses and in night-clubs, to the urbane business associate who had spoken to him like a teacher addressing an obtuse pupil.

'Do you want to see him?'

The prosecutor, a highly dignified magistrate from an old noble family, said:

'I've phoned the Foreign Ministry. David Ward really was an important figure. He was a colonel because of his war service at the head of a branch of Intelligence. Do you think that may have a connection with his death?'

Footsteps in the corridor, a knock at the door, and at last Doctor Paul appeared, carrying his instrument case.

'I thought for a minute they were going to make me come in through the service entrance. They're doing that right now to the people from Criminal Records. Where's the body?'

He shook hands with the prosecutor, then Calas, the new examining magistrate, and finally Maigret.

'So what is it, my friend?'

He took off his jacket and rolled up his shirt-sleeves.

'A man or a woman?'

'A man.'

Maigret pointed the doctor to the bathroom and heard him let out a cry. The men from Criminal Records now arrived with their equipment, and Maigret had to deal with them.

At the George-V as elsewhere, for David Ward as for any crime victim, they had to follow procedure.

'Can we open the shutters, chief?'

'Yes. Don't bother with this glass. It was just brought up for a witness.'

By now, the sun was flooding not only the sitting room but the huge, bright bedroom, too, revealing a large number of personal belongings, almost all rare or valuable.

The alarm clock on the bedside table, for instance, was made of gold and came from Cartier's, as did the cigar box on the chest of drawers, while the manicure set bore the brand name of a leading company based in London.

In the wardrobe, one of the men counted eighteen suits, and no doubt there were just as many in Ward's other suites, in Cannes, Lausanne and London.

'You can send in the photographer,' Doctor Paul called out.

Maigret was looking everywhere and nowhere, registering the slightest details of the suite and what was in it.

'Phone Lucas and ask if he has any news,' he said to Lapointe, who seemed a little lost in all the hubbub.

There were three telephones, one in the sitting room, another by the bed, the third in the bathroom.

'Hello, Lucas? Lapointe here.'

By the window, Maigret was conferring in a low voice with the prosecutor and the examining magistrate. Doctor Paul and the photographer were in the bathroom, where they couldn't be seen.

'We'll see if Doctor Paul confirms what Dr Frère said. According to him, the bruises . . .'

Doctor Paul appeared at last, as jovial as ever.

'You'll have to wait for my report, and probably the

post-mortem, because I assume there'll be one, but what I can tell you now is this. Firstly, with a constitution like that, the fellow could have lived until at least eighty. Secondly, he was fairly drunk when he got in the bath. Thirdly, he didn't slip, and whoever gave him a helping hand had to work quite hard to keep his head underwater. That's all I can say for the moment. If you want to send him to me at the Forensic Institute, I'll try to find out more . . .'

The prosecutor and the examining magistrate exchanged glances. Should they order a post-mortem or not?

'Does he have family?' the prosecutor asked Maigret.

'From what I gather, he had two children, both minors, and his divorce from his third wife wasn't yet final.'

'Brothers and sisters?'

'Just a moment . . .'

He picked up the telephone again. Lapointe was signalling to him that he had something to tell him, but first Maigret asked for the bar.

'Monsieur Arnold, please.'

'One moment . . .'

Soon afterwards, Maigret announced to the prosecutor:

'No sisters. He had one brother, who was killed in India at the age of twenty-two. There are also a few cousins, but he never kept up relations with them . . . What was it you wanted, Lapointe?'

'Lucas told me something he'd just heard. At about nine o'clock this morning, Countess Palmieri called from her room and asked for several telephone numbers.'

'Was a record kept of them?'

'Not those in Paris. There were two or three of them, apparently, including one she called twice. Then she called Monte Carlo.'

'What number?'

'The Hôtel de Paris.'

'Do we know who she called?'

'No. Do you want me to get through to the Hôtel de Paris?'

It was all still within the same world. Here, the George-V. In Monte Carlo, the most luxurious hotel on the Riviera.

'Hello, mademoiselle? Can you get me the Hôtel de Paris in Monte Carlo, please? . . . What?'

He turned, embarrassed, to Maigret.

'She's asking whose account she should put the call on.'

'On Ward's,' Maigret replied impatiently. 'Or mine, if she prefers.'

'Hello, mademoiselle? . . . It's for Detective Chief Inspector Maigret . . . Yes . . . Thank you.'

He put the phone down and announced:

'Ten minutes to wait.'

In a drawer, they had found letters, some in English, others in French or Italian, all jumbled up, letters from women and business letters mixed together, invitations to cocktail parties and dinners. In another drawer were files, in a more regular order.

'Shall we take them away?'

Maigret looked questioningly at Judge Calas and then nodded. It was eleven o'clock, and the hotel was starting to wake up, you could hear bells ringing, valets and chambermaids coming and going, the constant clatter of the lift.

'Do you think, doctor, that a woman could have held his head under the water?'

'It depends on the woman.'

'They call her the little countess, which suggests she's rather small.'

'It isn't the height or the girth that counts,' Doctor Paul grunted philosophically.

'It might be a good idea to have a look at 332,' Maigret said.

'332?'

'The countess's suite.'

Finding the door closed, they had to go in search of a chambermaid. The suite, which also comprised a sitting room, smaller than the one in 347, a bedroom and a bathroom, had already been cleaned.

Although the window was open, a smell of perfume and alcohol lingered in the air. The bottle of champagne had been removed, but the whisky bottle was still on the pedestal table, three-quarters empty.

The prosecutor and the examining magistrate, being too well brought up or too shy, stopped in the doorway, while Maigret opened cupboards and drawers. What he discovered was a feminine version of what he had discovered in David Ward's suite, expensive objects that are only found in a few shops and are like the symbols of a certain lifestyle.

On the dressing table, jewellery lay about as if it were of little value: a diamond bracelet with a tiny watch, rings and earrings worth some twenty million francs in all.

Here too, papers in a drawer, invitations, bills from dressmakers and milliners, leaflets, Air France and Pan Am timetables.

No personal letters, as if the little countess neither received nor wrote correspondence. What Maigret did find, in a closet, was twenty-eight pairs of shoes, some of which had never been worn. Their size confirmed that the countess really was small.

Lapointe came running.

'I just spoke to the Hôtel de Paris. The switchboard operator notes the calls the guests make, but not the ones they receive, except when they're away and she has to take a message. There were more than fifteen calls from Paris this morning, and she can't say who this one was for.'

Lapointe hesitated, then added:

'She asked me if it was as hot here as it is down there. Apparently . . .'

But nobody was listening to him any more, and he fell silent. The little group set off back to David Ward's suite and on the way encountered a rather strange procession. The manager, who had doubtless been alerted, was at the head of it, like a scout, keeping an anxious eye on the doors, which might open at any moment. He had brought along one of the blue-uniformed bellboys to clear the way.

Four men followed, carrying the stretcher on which David Ward's body, still naked, lay hidden by a blanket.

'This way,' Monsieur Gilles said in a muted voice.

He was walking on tiptoe. The bearers advanced cautiously, trying not to hit the walls and doors.

They headed, not for one of the main lifts, but for a corridor that was narrower than the others, with less bright, less new paint, which led to the goods lift.

David Ward, who had been one of the hotel's most prestigious guests, was leaving it by the route reserved for trunks and other large items of luggage.

There was a silence. The prosecutor and the examining magistrate, who had nothing more to do, were reluctant to go back into the suite.

The prosecutor sighed. 'You deal with it, Maigret.' Then he hesitated, and said in a lower voice: 'Handle this with care. Try to make sure the papers don't . . . Well, you know what I mean. The ministry was clear about that.'

How much less complicated it had been the day before, round about the same time, when Maigret had gone to Rue de Clignancourt to pay a visit to the debt collector, a father of three, who had been shot twice in the stomach while trying to protect his bag containing eight million francs.

He had refused to be taken to hospital. If he was going to die, he preferred to do so in the little room with the pink-flowered wallpaper where his wife watched over him and the children, when they got back from school, walked on tiptoe.

In that case, they had a lead, the beret that had been left on the premises, which was sure to lead them to the culprits in the end.

But in the case of David Ward?

'I think I'll go over to Orly,' Maigret said suddenly, as if talking to himself.

Was it because of the Air France and PanAm timetables left in the drawer, or because of the telephone call to Monte Carlo?

Or was it because he had to do something, anything, and an airport seemed in line with a person like the countess?

3.

Concerning the little countess's comings and goings and Maigret's qualms

He was not to leave the George-V as quickly as he had intended. As he was giving instructions to Lucas by telephone before going to the airport, young Lapointe, who had gone to take another look around Countess Palmieri's bedroom, brought back a coloured metal tin, originally for English biscuits, now stuffed full of photographs.

It reminded Maigret of the tin his mother had used for buttons when he was small, into which she dipped every time a button was missing from a garment. That one was a tea tin, decorated with Chinese characters, which was an unusual thing to find in the house of an estate manager who never drank tea.

In a closet in 332, Maigret had seen suitcases from a famous luggage shop on Avenue Marceau, and even the small everyday objects, a shoe horn, a paperweight, were luxury brands.

And yet it was in a simple biscuit tin that the countess kept, in no particular order, photographs of herself and her friends, snapshots taken on her travels, showing her in a swimming costume on board a yacht, somewhere in the Mediterranean probably, or water-skiing, or somewhere in the mountains, surrounded by snow.

In some of the photographs, she was accompanied by the colonel, sometimes alone with him, most often with other people whom Maigret recognized as actors, writers, people whose pictures were often in the newspapers.

'Are you taking the tin with you, chief?'

It was as if Maigret were reluctant to leave this floor of the George-V even though there seemed to be nothing more to be learned.

'Call the nurse. But make sure it's the same one as last night.'

It was the same, for the good reason that there was only one attached to the hotel. Her main tasks, Maigret was to learn somewhat later, were to treat hangovers and give injections. For a few years now, a third of the guests, on their doctors' orders, had been getting injections of one kind or another.

'Tell me, Mademoiselle . . .'

'Genévrier.'

She was a sad, dignified woman of indeterminate age, with the dull eyes of those who don't get enough sleep.

'When Countess Palmieri left the hotel by ambulance, she was in her nightdress, am I right?'

'Yes. We wrapped her in a blanket. I didn't want to waste any time dressing her. I put some clothes and underwear in a suitcase.'

'Including a dress?'

'A blue tailored suit, the first thing I found. Shoes and stockings, too, of course.'

48

'Anything else?'

'A handbag, which was in the bedroom. I made sure it contained a comb, a compact, lipstick, everything a woman needs.'

'Do you know if there was any money in the handbag?'

'I saw a purse, a chequebook and a passport.'

'A French passport?'

'Italian.'

'Is the countess Italian?'

'French. She became Italian through her marriage to Count Palmieri, and I assume she held on to Italian nationality. I don't know. I don't have anything to do with that kind of thing.'

In the lift, there was a man Lapointe couldn't stop staring at, whom Maigret eventually recognized as the greatest American film comedian. It was strange, after seeing him so often on the screen, to encounter him in the flesh, in a lift, dressed like anybody else, with bags under his eyes and the glum air of someone who drank too much the night before.

Instead of heading for the lobby, Maigret dropped into the bar, where John T. Arnold was sitting over a whisky.

'Would you mind coming over here for a moment?'

There were still only a few customers, most looking as sallow as the American actor, except for two who had spread business documents on a pedestal table and were engaged in a serious discussion.

Maigret passed the photographs to Arnold, one at a time.

'I assume you know these people? I noticed you're in some of these pictures yourself.'

Arnold did indeed know all of them. Many were figures whose names were known to Maigret, too: two former kings who had once ruled their countries and now lived on the Riviera, an ex-queen who lived in Lausanne, a few princes, a British film director, the owner of a major brand of whisky, a ballerina, a tennis champion.

There was something a little annoying about the way Arnold spoke of them.

'Don't you recognize him? That's Paul.'

'Paul who?'

'Paul of Yugoslavia. This one's Nénette.'

Nénette wasn't the nickname of an actress or a demi-mondaine, but of a lady who received ministers and ambassadors for dinner in her apartment on Faubourg Saint-Germain.

'What about this one who's with the countess and the colonel?'

'Jef.'

'Jef who?'

'Van Meulen, the chemicals man.'

Another name Maigret knew, of course, one you found on cans of paint and many other products.

He was in shorts and a huge straw hat, like a South American planter, and was playing bowls on a square in Saint-Tropez.

'He's the countess's second husband.'

'One more question, Monsieur Arnold. Do you know anyone who's currently staying at the Hôtel de Paris in Monte Carlo whom the countess might have tried to telephone if she was in trouble?'

'She phoned Monte Carlo?'

'I asked you a question.'

'Jef, of course.'

'You mean her second husband?'

'He spends quite a lot of the year on the Riviera. He owns a villa in Mougins, near Cannes, but most of the time he prefers the Hôtel de Paris.'

'Have they stayed on good terms?'

'Excellent terms. She still calls him Daddy.'

The American comedian, having strolled around the lobby, now came and stood at the bar. He wasn't asked what he wanted, but was automatically presented with a large glass of gin and tomato juice.

'Were Van Meulen and the colonel on good terms?'

'They were old friends.'

'What about Count Palmieri?'

'He's in one of the photographs you've just shown me.'

Arnold picked it out. A tall, dark young man with thick hair, in swimming trunks in the bow of a yacht.

'Another friend?'

'Why not?'

'Many thanks . . .'

Maigret was about to stand, then changed his mind.

'Do you know who the colonel's notary is?'

John T. Arnold again appeared somewhat impatient, as if Maigret were far too ignorant.

'He has a lot of them. Not necessarily notaries as you French think of them. In London, his solicitors are Messrs Philps, Philps and Hadley. In New York, the firm of Harrison and Shaw handles his affairs. In Lausanne—'

'With which of these gentlemen do you think he placed his will?'

'He's left wills everywhere. He kept changing them.'

Maigret had accepted the whisky he had been offered but Lapointe, discreetly, had taken only a glass of beer.

'Many thanks, Monsieur Arnold.'

'Please don't forget what I told you. Handle with care. There are bound to be complications . . .'

Maigret was all too well aware of this, and it wasn't putting him in a good mood. He was irritated by all these people whose customs were so different from those of ordinary mortals. He was starting to realize that he was ill prepared to understand them and that it would take months to become fully conversant with their affairs.

'Come, Lapointe.'

He hurried across the lobby without looking right or left, for fear of being buttonholed by Monsieur Gilles – he liked the man well enough, but he, too, would be sure to advise caution and discretion. By now the lobby was almost filled to bursting with people speaking every language under the sun and smoking cigarettes and cigars from around the world.

'This way, Monsieur Maigret . . .'

The doorman led them to the place where he had parked the small police car, between a Rolls and a Cadillac.

Tip? No tip? Maigret didn't give one.

'Let's go to Orly, son.'

'Yes, chief.'

Maigret would have liked to go to the American Hospital in Neuilly and question the nurse, the receptionist, the switchboard operator. There were lots of things he'd have liked to do, things he should be doing. But he couldn't be everywhere at once and he was anxious to track down the little countess, as her friends called her.

And she was indeed little, she was slight and pretty, as he knew from her photographs. How old could she be? It was hard to say. Most of the snapshots had been taken in bright sunlight, giving a better idea of her body, almost naked in a bikini, than the details of her features.

She had brown hair, a cheeky little pointed nose and sparkling eyes, and liked to pose as a mischievous young thing.

He would have sworn, though, that she was pushing forty. The hotel records would have told him for sure, but he hadn't thought of it earlier. He was going too fast, with the disagreeable impression that he was sabotaging his own investigation.

'I'd like you to go to the George-V later and get her registration form,' he said to Lapointe. 'Then have the clearest of the photographs enlarged.'

'Are we putting it in the newspapers?'

'Not yet. I also want you to go to the American Hospital. Have you got all that?'

'Yes. Are you leaving?'

It wasn't certain yet, but he had the feeling he was.

'If I do go, telephone my wife.'

He had travelled by plane four or five times, but that had been a while back, and he barely recognized Orly, where there were new buildings and the whole place was busier than Gare du Nord or Gare Saint-Lazare, for instance.

The difference was that here, it was as if you were still at the George-V, you heard every language under the sun being spoken and saw tips given in every imaginable currency. Press photographers, gathered around a large car, were taking pictures of a woman celebrity whose arms were laden with flowers, and most of the suitcases were the same prestigious brand as those of the little countess.

'Shall I wait for you, chief?'

'No. Go back to town and do what I told you. If I don't leave, I'll take a taxi back.'

He edged his way into the crowd in order to avoid the reporters and, by the time he got to the concourse, where the desks of the various airlines stood in a row, two planes had landed and a number of Indians, some in turbans, were crossing the tarmac in the direction of customs.

There were constant messages coming from the loud-speakers.

'Mr Stillwell is asked to go to the PanAm desk . . . Mr Stillwell is asked to go . . .'

Then the same announcement in English, and another in Spanish, addressed to someone named Consuelo Gonzalez.

The office of the special chief inspector for the airport was no longer where Maigret remembered it. He found it in the end, however, and opened the door.

'There you are, Colombani!'

Colombani, whose wedding Maigret had attended, wasn't part of the Police Judiciaire, but answered directly to the Ministry of the Interior.

'Was it you who sent this through to me?'

Chief Inspector Colombani looked through the mess on his desk for the piece of paper on which the countess's name was written in pencil.

'Have you seen her?'

'I passed it on to the security people. I haven't heard anything from them so far. Let me check the passenger lists . . .'

He went into the adjoining office, which had glass walls, and came back with a bundle of papers.

'Let's see now . . . Flight 315 to London . . . Palmieri . . . Palmieri . . . P . . . No, no Palmieris among the passengers . . . Do you have any idea where she went? . . . The next plane was Stuttgart . . . No Palmieri there either . . . Cairo, Beirut . . . P . . . Potteret . . . No! . . . PanAm to New York . . . There's a Pittsberg, a Piroulet . . . Still no Palmieri . . .'

'Were there any planes for the Riviera?'

'Yes, the 10.32 plane for Rome stops in Nice.'

'Do you have the passenger list?'

'I have a list of the Rome passengers, because my men checked their passports. They don't bother with the people going to Nice, who don't go in through the same gate and don't have to pass through customs and police checks.'

'Is it a French plane?'

'British. You'll need to speak to BOAC. I'll take you there.'

The desks on the concourse were lined up like fairground stalls, with signs above them in the colours of the different countries, almost all of them bearing mysterious sets of initials.

'Do you have a list of passengers on Flight 312?'

The freckled English girl looked in her files and held out a sheet of paper.

'P . . . P . . . Parsons . . . Palmieri . . . Louise, Countess Palmieri . . . That the one, Maigret?'

'Could you tell me if this passenger had pre-booked her seat?' Maigret asked the girl.

'Hold on a moment. It was my colleague who was here for that flight.'

She left her booth, plunged into the crowd and eventually returned with a tall, fair-haired young man who spoke French with a strong accent.

'Was it you who made out Countess Palmieri's ticket?'

He said yes. His neighbour from Alitalia had brought her over. She absolutely had to get to Nice and had missed the morning's Air France flight.

'It's complicated, you know. There are airlines that only fly a particular route once or twice a week. On some routes, the stops aren't always the same either. I told her that if we had a seat at the last minute—'

'Did she get on the plane?'

'Yes. The 10.32.'

'So she should be in Nice by now?'

He looked at a clock above the desk opposite.

'She arrived half an hour ago.'

'How did she pay for her ticket?'

'By cheque. She told me she'd left in a hurry and didn't have any money on her.'

'Do you usually accept cheques?'

'When it's people we know.'

'Do you still have hers?'

He opened a drawer, fiddled with a few papers and took out a sheet to which a blueish cheque was pinned. The cheque hadn't been drawn on a French bank, but a Swiss bank that had a branch on Avenue de l'Opéra. The handwriting was nervous and irregular, the handwriting of someone who was very impatient or in a feverish state.

'Many thanks.' He turned to Colombani. 'Can I call Nice from your office?'

'You can even send a message by telex and it'll be received instantaneously.'

'I'd rather speak to someone.'

'Come with me. Is it an important case?'

'Very!'

'But an awkward one?'

'Unfortunately, yes.'

'Is it the airport police you want to speak to?'

Maigret nodded.

'It'll take a few minutes to get through. We have time for a drink. This way . . . Will you let us know when we have Nice on the line, Dutilleul?'

At the bar, they squeezed in between a Brazilian family and a group of grey-uniformed pilots speaking French with Belgian or Swiss accents.

'What'll you have?'

'I just had a whisky. I might as well have the same again.'

'The message we got from the Police Judiciaire didn't mention passengers for a French airport,' Colombani said.

'As we usually only deal with those who have to show their passports . . .'

Maigret was already being called to the telephone, so he knocked his drink back in one go.

'Hello, airport police? . . . Maigret here, from the Police Judiciaire . . . Yes . . . Can you hear me? . . . I'm speaking as clearly as I can . . . A young woman named Countess Palmieri . . . Like palm . . . The trees on the Promenade des Anglais . . . With *ieri* at the end . . . Yes . . . She probably got off the BOAC plane just over half an hour ago . . . Yes, the plane from London via Paris . . . What? . . . I can't hear . . .'

Colombani kindly went and shut the door to block out the din of the airport, including the noise of a plane approaching the vast picture windows.

'The plane has only just landed? . . . A delay, yes . . . All the better . . . So the passengers are still in the airport? . . . If you're quick about it . . . Palmieri . . . No, just find some excuse to hold on to her. Her papers need checking, something like that . . . But be quick.'

'I thought there might be a delay,' Colombani said, accustomed to such things. 'They're reporting storms all along that route. The plane from Casablanca was an hour and a half late and the one from—'

'Hello? . . . Yes . . . What? . . . You saw her? . . . And? . . . She's gone?'

At the other end of the line, too, engine noises could be heard.

'Is that the plane leaving now? . . . Is she on it? . . . No?'

He finally understood that the officer in Nice had just

missed her. The passengers who had come from London were still there, because they had to pass through customs, but the countess, who had got on in Paris, had been first out and had immediately climbed into a waiting car.

'A car with a Belgian number plate, you say? . . . Yes, I heard that: a large car with a chauffeur . . . No, nothing . . . Thank you.'

From the American Hospital, she had telephoned Monte Carlo, where her second husband, Joseph Van Meulen, was probably at the Hôtel de Paris. Then she'd had herself driven to Orly and had taken the first plane for the Riviera. In Nice, a large Belgian car had been waiting for her.

'Is everything going the way you hoped?' Colombani asked.

'When's the next plane for Nice?'

'The 13.19. In principle, they're full, even though it's not the season. At the last minute, though, there are always one or two passengers who don't show up. Do you want me to book you on it?'

Without him, Maigret would have wasted a lot of time.

'Done! Now all you have to do is wait. We'll come and get you when it's time. Will you be in the restaurant?'

Maigret had lunch alone in a corner, after phoning Lucas, who had nothing new to tell him.

'Are the press on to it yet?'

'I don't think so. I saw one reporter prowling the corridors earlier, but it was Michaux, who always hangs around, and he didn't say anything to me.'

'Make sure Lapointe does what I told him. I'll call from Nice some time this afternoon.'

They came for him as promised, and he followed the line of passengers on to the plane, where he sat down in the last row. He had handed the tin of photographs over to Lapointe, but had kept a few that struck him as the most interesting and, instead of reading the newspaper that the stewardess offered him along with some chewing gum, he began looking through them pensively.

To smoke his pipe and loosen his belt, he had to wait for a sign in front of him to go out. Almost immediately, tea and cakes were served, but he didn't want any.

Eyes half-closed, head tilted against the back of his seat, he seemed not to be thinking, as the plane flew over a thick carpet of bright clouds. In reality, he was making an effort to bring names and shadowy figures to life, names and figures that even this morning had been as unknown to him as the inhabitants of another planet.

How long would it be before the death of the colonel became known and the press seized on the story? That was when the complications would start, as always happened in a case involving celebrities. Would the London papers send reporters to Paris? If John T. Arnold was to be believed, David Ward had business interests all over the world.

What a curious character! Maigret had only seen him in a pitiful, grotesque position, naked in his bath, with his big pale belly seeming to float on the surface of the water.

Had Lapointe sensed that Maigret was overwhelmed, not quite up to the task, and had his confidence in his chief been shaken?

These people irritated him, that much was a fact. Faced

with them, he was in the position of a newcomer in a club, for example, or a new pupil in a class who feels awkward and embarrassed because he doesn't yet know the rules, the customs, the catchphrases, and assumes that the others are laughing at him.

He was convinced that John T. Arnold, so relaxed and comfortable with bankers and exiled kings in London, Rome, Berlin or New York, had been amused by Maigret's awkwardness and had treated him with a somewhat pitying condescension.

Maigret knew as well as anybody, and better than most because of his profession, how some kinds of business were conducted and how people in certain circles lived.

But it was a theoretical knowledge. He didn't 'feel' it. All sorts of details threw him.

It was the first time he'd had occasion to deal with this world apart, which you only heard about through gossip in the press.

There were billionaires, to use the accepted term, who were easy to place, whose lives could be more or less imagined, businessmen or bankers who went to their offices every day and who, in private, didn't seem any different from ordinary mortals.

He had known major industrialists in the north and the east, owners of wool mills or ironworks, who were at their desks by eight o'clock every morning, in bed by ten every night, and whose families were similar to those of their department heads or their foremen.

Now he was starting to realize that people like that

weren't quite at the top of the ladder, that where the rich were concerned, they were merely wage-earners.

Above them were men like Colonel Ward, perhaps like Joseph Van Meulen, who virtually never set foot in an office, going from one luxury hotel to another, surrounded by pretty women, cruising on their yachts, maintaining complicated relationships among themselves and conducting business, even in hotel lobbies or nightclubs, that brought in much more than any bourgeois financier ever handled.

David Ward had had three wives, whose names Maigret had written down in his black notebook. Dorothy Payne, the first, was the only one to belong to more or less the same background as him, the only one who was also from Manchester. They hadn't had children and had divorced after three years. She had remarried.

Her family may have been bourgeois, but she hadn't returned to that world after her divorce and had never gone back to Manchester. She had, in a way, married another Ward, a man named Aldo de Rocca, an artificial silks tycoon in Italy, who was crazy about cars and took part in the 24 Hours at Le Mans every year.

Aldo de Rocca, too, probably stayed at the George-V or the Ritz, the Savoy in London, the Carlton in Cannes, the Hôtel de Paris in Monte Carlo.

How could these people avoid meeting one another constantly? There were twenty or thirty top-class hotels in the world, a dozen fashionable beach resorts, a limited number of galas, Grand Prix and Derbys. All these people used the same jewellers, couturiers, tailors. The same hairdressers, too, even the same manicurists.

The colonel's second wife, Alice Perrin, whose son was in Cambridge, was from a different background, since she was the daughter of a village teacher in the Nièvre and had been working as a model in Paris when Ward met her.

But didn't models live somewhat on the edges of the same world?

After her divorce, she hadn't gone back to her former work, and the colonel had provided her with a private income.

What kind of people was she mixing with now?

The same thing could be asked of the third – Muriel Halligan, daughter of a foreman from Hoboken, New Jersey, who had been selling cigarettes in a Broadway nightclub when David Ward had fallen in love with her.

She now lived in Lausanne with her daughter, equally free of money worries.

Incidentally, was John T. Arnold married? Maigret would have sworn he wasn't. He seemed born to be the factotum, the éminence grise, the confidant of a man like Ward. He probably belonged to a good English family, perhaps a very old family that had suffered reverses of fortune. He had studied at Eton and Cambridge and practised golf, tennis, sailing and rowing. Quite likely, before meeting Ward, he had been in the army or the diplomatic corps.

He might have been in the colonel's shadow, but he certainly led the life he was meant for. It was even possible that he took discreet advantage of his patron's love affairs, as he did of his wealth.

'Ladies and gentlemen, may we ask you to fasten your seat belts and stop smoking. We will shortly be landing in Nice. We hope you have had a pleasant flight.'

Maigret had difficulty emptying his pipe in the tiny ashtray embedded in the arm of his seat and loosening the buckle of his belt with his thick fingers. He hadn't noticed that for a short while now they had been flying over the sea. It appeared suddenly in the window, almost vertically, as the plane was banking. There were fishing boats that looked like toys and a two-masted yacht that left a silvery trail in its wake.

'Please don't leave your seats until the plane has come to a complete stop.'

The plane touched down, bouncing a little, and the engines grew louder as it taxied to the white airport building. Maigret's ears were humming.

Maigret was one of the last to get off, because he was right at the back, and a fat lady ahead of him had left a box of chocolates on her seat and laboriously worked her way back through the line of passengers.

At the foot of the steps, a young man without a jacket, his shirt dazzling in the sun, touched his straw hat and said:

'Detective Chief Inspector Maigret?'

'Yes.'

'Inspector Benoît. I wasn't the one who got your message at midday, that was my colleague, but I've relieved him. The airport chief inspector apologizes for not being here to welcome you. He's been called to town on an important case.'

At a distance, he followed the passengers rushing to the buildings. The concrete of the runway was hot. Behind a barrier, you could see a crowd of people waving handkerchieves in the sun.

'We were quite embarrassed about what happened. I asked the chief's advice and took the liberty of phoning Quai des Orfèvres. I spoke to someone named Lucas, and he told me he knew all about it. The woman you're interested in . . .'

He looked at a piece of paper he had been holding in his hand.

'. . . Countess Palmieri came back just in time to catch a Swissair plane. As we had no instructions, I didn't dare detain her off my own bat. The chief wasn't sure what to do either. So I called the Police Judiciaire urgently and Inspector Lucas—'

'Sergeant.'

'I'm sorry, Sergeant Lucas seemed as put out as I was. The woman wasn't alone. There was an important-looking man with her who had brought her in his car and had phoned half an hour earlier to book her a seat on the plane to Geneva.'

'Van Meulen?'

'I don't know. They'll be able to tell you in the office.'

'In other words, you let her go again?'

'Did I do the wrong thing?'

Maigret did not reply immediately.

'No. I don't think so,' he said at last with a sigh. 'When's the next plane to Geneva?'

'There isn't one until tomorrow morning. If you

absolutely have to go there, there is another way. Just the day before yesterday, there was someone in the same situation. By taking the 20.40 plane to Rome, you get there in time to catch the Rome–Geneva–Paris–London and—'

Maigret almost burst out laughing. He suddenly had the impression he was behind the times. To get from Nice to Geneva, all you had to do was go to Rome, and from there . . .

In the bar, just as at Orly, he saw pilots and stewardesses, Americans, Italians, Spaniards. A four-year-old boy, who had been travelling on his own from New York, passed from one stewardess to another, was solemnly eating an ice cream.

'I'd like to make a telephone call.'

The inspector admitted him to the cramped police office, where they already knew who he was and looked at him with great curiosity.

'What number, detective chief inspector?'

'The Hôtel de Paris in Monte Carlo.'

Within a few moments he had learned from the porter of the Hôtel de Paris that Monsieur Joseph Van Meulen did indeed have a suite at the hotel, that he had been called to Nice by a telephone call, that his chauffeur had driven him there and that he had been away for quite a long time and had only just got back.

Right now he was having a bath. He had a table booked for the gala dinner at the Sporting Club that very evening.

They hadn't seen Countess Palmieri, who was very well known in the hotel. As for Mademoiselle Nadine, she hadn't gone with Van Meulen when he had left in his car.

Who was Nadine? Maigret had no idea. The porter, though, seemed convinced the whole world knew who she was, and Maigret avoided asking any questions.

'Are you taking the Rome plane?' the young inspector asked.

'No. I'll book a seat on Swissair for tomorrow morning. I'll probably spend the night in Monte Carlo.'

'I'll take you to Swissair.'

A desk on the concourse, side by side with other desks.

'Do you know Countess Palmieri?'

'She's one of our best customers. She took a plane for Geneva not long ago.'

'Do you know where she's staying in Geneva?'

'She doesn't usually stay in Geneva, but in Lausanne. We've often sent her tickets at the Lausanne Palace.'

It suddenly struck Maigret that Paris was so large and the world so small! It took him almost as long to get to Monte Carlo by coach as it had taken him to fly here from Orly.

4.

In which Maigret meets another billionaire, as naked as the colonel, but alive and well

Here, too, there was no desire to advertise the presence of the police. Entering the lobby, Maigret recognized the porter, whom he had phoned from the airport and with whom, he realized on seeing him, he had several times had dealings when the man worked in a luxury hotel on the Champs-Élysées. At that time, he hadn't presided over the key rack, nor had he worn this long frock coat, but had been a mere bellboy at the guests' beck and call.

In the lobby, there were still people in beachwear as well as men already in dinner jackets. A large, almost naked woman in front of Maigret, her back scarlet, a little dog under her arm, gave off a strong smell of suntan oil.

Instead of calling Maigret by his name – let alone addressing him as detective chief inspector! – the porter gave him a conspiratorial wink and said:

'Just a moment . . . Yes, I've taken care of it.'

Then he picked up the telephone.

'Hello, Monsieur Jean?'

He spoke in a low voice: the telephones must have been particularly sensitive here.

'The person I told you about has arrived. Should I send him up? . . . Of course.'

Then, to Maigret:

'Monsieur Van Meulen's secretary is waiting for you on the fifth floor, outside the lift, and he'll take you . . .'

It was rather as if they were doing him a favour. A young man dressed up to the nines was indeed waiting for him in the corridor.

'Monsieur Joseph Van Meulen has asked me to apologize for seeing you during his massage, but he has to go out almost immediately afterwards. He's also asked me to tell you that he's delighted to meet you in the flesh. He's followed some of your cases with enormous interest.'

It was all a little odd. Why couldn't Van Meulen tell him these things himself, since they were about to find themselves face to face?

Maigret was admitted to a suite so similar to the one in the George-V – the same furniture, an identical layout – that he might have thought himself still in Paris if he hadn't seen the harbour and the yachts through the windows.

'Detective Chief Inspector Maigret,' Monsieur Jean announced, opening the door to the bedroom.

'Come in, detective chief inspector, make yourself at home,' said a man lying on his stomach, stark naked, being kneaded by a masseur in white trousers and a vest that left his huge biceps uncovered. 'I've been expecting a visit, but I assumed they would just send me a local inspector. That you went to all this trouble personally . . .'

He didn't finish the sentence. He was the second billionaire Maigret had encountered in one day and was as naked as the first, although that didn't seem to embarrass him in the least.

In the photographs found in the biscuit tin, many of the people were barely dressed, as if, above a certain social level, there were a different notion of modesty.

The man was probably very tall and still quite slim. He was tanned all over except for a narrow strip of skin that his swimming trunks had prevented from absorbing the sun and which was embarrassingly white. Maigret couldn't see his face, which was buried in the pillow, but the skull, equally tanned, was bald and smooth.

Heedless of the masseur's presence – he was probably of no importance in his eyes – Van Meulen continued:

'I knew, of course, that you would track down Louise. I advised her this morning, on the telephone, that she shouldn't try to hide. Mind you, I didn't know at that point what had happened. She didn't dare give me the details over the phone. Besides, she was in such a state . . . Have you met her?'

'No.'

'She's a strange creature, one of the oddest and most endearing women there are . . . Have you finished yet, Bob?'

'Two more minutes, monsieur.'

The masseur, with his broken nose and squashed ears, must once have been a boxer. His forearms and the backs of his hands were covered with jet-black hairs on which sweat had formed.

'I assume you're still in touch with Paris? What's the latest news?'

The man was speaking quite naturally, with a relaxed air.

'The investigation is still in its early stages,' Maigret replied cautiously.

'I'm not talking about the investigation. What about the papers? Have they published the story?'

'Not to my knowledge.'

'I'd be surprised if one of the Philpses at least, probably the younger of the two, hadn't already got on a plane for Paris.'

'Who would have informed them?'

'Arnold, of course. And as soon as the women find out . . .'

'Are you referring to the colonel's ex-wives?'

'This concerns them first and foremost, doesn't it? I have no idea where Dorothy is, but Alice must be in Paris, and Muriel, who lives in Lausanne, will jump on the first plane . . . That's enough, Bob. Thank you. Same time tomorrow . . . No, wait, I have an appointment! Shall we say four o'clock?'

The masseur had placed a yellow terry towel over the middle part of Van Meulen's body, and Van Meulen stood up slowly, wrapping the towel around himself like a loin-cloth. Standing, he was indeed very tall, strong and muscular, in perfect physical condition for a man of sixty-five, perhaps even seventy. He looked at Maigret with a curiosity he made no attempt to conceal.

'It gives me great pleasure . . .' he said, without going into further details. 'I hope you don't mind if I get dressed in front of you? I have to, I've invited twenty people to the gala dinner this evening. I just have time to take a shower . . .'

He went into the bathroom, and water could be heard running. The masseur put his things away in a small case, donned a coloured jacket and left after also throwing Maigret a curious glance.

Van Meulen was already back, wrapped in a dressing gown, drops of water on his skull and face. His dinner suit, his white silk shirt, socks, shoes, everything he was going to wear was together on an ingenious clothes stand the like of which Maigret had never seen before.

'David was a good friend, an old partner in crime, I might say. We'd known each other for more than thirty years – no, wait, thirty-eight years exactly – and we'd been equal partners in quite a few business deals. I was very surprised by the news of his death, especially a death like that.'

The surprising thing was how completely natural he was, so much so that Maigret couldn't recall having encountered anything like it in his life. He came and went, occupied with getting ready, and it was almost as if he were alone and talking to himself.

This was the man the little countess called 'Daddy', and Maigret was starting to understand why. You sensed his strength. You could rely on him. The young secretary was in the next room, making telephone calls. A waiter nobody had rung for brought in a misted glass containing a clear liquid, in all likelihood a Martini, on a silver tray. It must have been the hour for it, part of the daily routine.

'Thank you, Ludo. May I offer you something, Maigret?'

He didn't say 'detective chief inspector', or 'monsieur', and there was nothing shocking about that. It could even be seen as a way of putting the two of them on an equal footing.

'I'll have the same as you.'

'Very dry?'

Maigret nodded. Van Meulen had already put on trousers, vest and black silk socks and was looking around for his shoe horn so that he could put on his polished shoes.

'Have you ever met her?'

'You mean Countess Palmieri?'

'Louise, yes. If you don't yet know her, you may find this hard to understand. You have wide experience of men, I know, but I wonder if you understand women so well . . . Are you planning to go and see her in Lausanne?'

He wasn't playing any tricks, wasn't trying to pretend that the countess was anywhere else.

'She'll have had time to calm down a little. This morning, when she called me from the clinic, she was so incoherent that I advised her to get on the first plane she could and come to see me.'

'The two of you were married, weren't you?'

'Yes, for two and a half years. We've remained good friends. Why should we have fallen out? . . . It's a miracle that the nurse at the George-V thought of putting some clothes and Louise's handbag in the ambulance, otherwise she wouldn't have been able to leave the hospital. She had no money in her bag, just some small change. At Orly, she was forced to pay her taxi fare with a cheque, and that wasn't the only thing. Anyway, I had her picked up at the airport, and we had a bite to eat in Nice, where she told me the story.'

Maigret avoided asking any questions, preferring to let Van Meulen speak freely.

'I hope you don't suspect her of killing David?'

Receiving no reply, Van Meulen stiffened.

'That would be a bad mistake, Maigret, I tell you this as a friend. And first of all, allow me to ask a question. Are you sure that someone kept David's head underwater?'

'Who told you that?'

'Louise, of course.'

'So she saw him?'

'Yes, she saw him and wouldn't dream of denying it. Didn't you know that? . . . Jean, could you give me my cufflinks and my shirt front buttons?'

He was suddenly anxious.

'Listen, Maigret, I'd better put you in the picture, otherwise you might get the wrong idea, and I'd like to avoid Louise being bothered more than is necessary. She's still a little girl. She may be thirty-nine, but she's a child and she'll always be a child. That's very much part of her charm. It's also what's constantly got her into impossible situations.'

The secretary helped him to put on his platinum cufflinks, and Van Meulen sat down opposite Maigret, as if granting himself a moment's rest.

'Louise's father was a general, and her mother was minor provincial nobility. She was born in Morocco, I think, where her father was stationed, but she spent much of her youth in Nancy. She already wanted to live her own life and she eventually managed to persuade her parents to send her to Paris to study art history . . . Cheers!'

Maigret took a gulp of his Martini and looked around for a pedestal table to put his glass on.

'Put it on the floor, it doesn't matter where . . . She met an Italian, Count Marco Palmieri. It was love at first sight. Have you met Palmieri?'

'No.'

'You will.'

He seemed sure of that.

'He's a real count, but has no money. From what I know, when he met Louise he was living off the kindness of a middle-aged lady. Louise's parents in Nancy took a good deal of persuading. But she sweetened the pill somehow, and they finally gave their consent to the marriage. Let's call that the first chapter, the time when people started talking about the "little countess". They had an apartment in Passy, then a hotel room, an apartment again, lots of ups and downs, but they never stopped being seen at cocktail parties and receptions and in places where people amuse themselves.'

'Was Palmieri using his wife?'

Van Meulen frankly hesitated.

'No. Not in the way you think. She wouldn't have allowed that anyway. She was madly in love with him and she still is. It gets harder to understand, doesn't it? But it's the truth. I'm even convinced that Marco's in love with her, too, or that at any rate he can't do without her. All the same, they did quarrel. She left him three or four times after violent scenes, but never for more than a few days. Marco would just have to show up looking pale and haggard and beg forgiveness, and she'd fall into his arms again.'

'What did they live on?'

Van Meulen shrugged imperceptibly.

'You ask me that? What do so many people we shake hands with every day live on? It was during one of those bad patches that I met her. I felt sorry for her. I didn't think it was the life for her, she was worn out, I thought she'd soon wither in the hands of a man like Marco and, as I'd just divorced, I proposed to her.'

'Were you in love with her?'

Van Meulen looked at him without saying a word and his eyes seemed to be repeating the question.

'The same kind of thing,' he said at last, 'has happened several times in my life, as it happened to David. Does that answer your question? I make no secret of the fact that I had a conversation with Marco and gave him a large cheque to take a trip to South America.'

'And he agreed?'

'I have ways of persuading people.'

'I assume he'd committed a number of . . . indiscretions?'

A barely perceptible shrug.

'Louise was my wife for nearly three years, and I was quite happy with her.'

'But you knew she was still in love with Marco?'

Van Meulen's expression seemed to say:

'What of it?'

He continued:

'She went everywhere with me. I travel a lot. She met my friends, some of whom she already knew. There were difficult moments, of course, and even a few really bad quarrels . . . I think she had, and still has, a genuine affection for me. She called me Daddy, which doesn't shock me: after all, I am thirty years older than her.'

'Was it through you that she met David Ward?'

'Yes, it was through me, as you say.'

A little ironic gleam had appeared in his eyes.

'It wasn't David who took her away from me, but Marco, who came back one fine day, thin and wretched, and started spending his days on the pavement opposite looking like a stray dog. One evening, she threw herself in my arms, sobbing, and confessed that—'

The telephone had rung in the next room, and now the secretary, who had answered it, appeared in the doorway.

'Monsieur Philps on the line.'

'Donald or Herbert?'

'Donald.'

'What did I tell you? He's the younger one . . . Is he calling from Paris?'

'Yes.'

'Put him through to me here.'

He reached out his hand for the telephone. The conversation was conducted in English.

'Yes . . .' Van Meulen replied to whatever was asked at the other end. 'No . . . I don't know yet . . . Apparently there's no doubt about it . . . Detective Chief Inspector

Maigret, who's handling the case, is with me right now . . .
I'll certainly be going to Paris for the funeral, although
it's really inconvenient, because I was supposed to be leaving for Ceylon the day after tomorrow. Are you at the
George-V? . . . If I find out anything, I'll call you . . . No,
I'll be out this evening and won't be back until three in
the morning . . . Have a good evening.'

He looked at Maigret.

'There you go. Philps is on the spot, as I predicted. He's
very agitated. The English newspapers already know
about it, and he's being besieged by reporters . . . Where
was I? I really do have to finish getting dressed . . . My
ties, Jean.'

He was brought six bow ties to choose from. They all
looked identical, but he examined them carefully before
selecting one.

'What else could I have done? I told her I would divorce
her, and since I didn't want Marco to leave her penniless,
rather than give her a lump sum I settled a modest regular
income on her.'

'And you continued to see her socially?'

'I continued to see both of them. Does that surprise
you?'

He knotted his bow tie in front of the mirror, stretching
his neck so that his Adam's apple stood out.

'As was only to be expected, the scenes started all over
again. Then, one fine day, David divorced Muriel, and
now it was his turn to play the Good Samaritan.'

'But he didn't marry her?'

'He didn't have time. He was waiting for the divorce

proceedings to be over . . . Come to think of it, I wonder what's going to happen now. I don't know exactly what stage they'd reached, but if all the papers haven't been signed, it's quite possible that Muriel Halligan will be considered David's widow.'

'Is this all that you know?'

'No,' Van Meulen replied simply. 'I also know at least some of what happened last night, and it might as well be me telling you as Louise. Before anything else, I want to make it quite clear that she didn't kill David Ward. First of all, she's probably incapable of it.'

'Physically, you mean?'

'Yes, that is what I mean. Morally, if I may use the expression, we're all capable of committing murder, provided we have sufficient motive and we're convinced we won't get caught.'

'Sufficient motive?'

'Passion, first of all. We're obliged to believe that, since every day we see men and women committing crimes of passion. Although if you want my opinion . . . Well, never mind! . . . Then there's financial gain. If someone stands to benefit from another person's death . . . But that's certainly not the case with Louise, quite the contrary.'

'Unless Ward made a will leaving everything to her, or—'

'There's no will leaving everything to her, believe me. David's an Englishman, which means he's level-headed and sees everything for what it is.'

'Was he in love with the countess?'

Van Meulen frowned irritably.

'That's the third or fourth time you've used that word, Maigret. Please try to understand. David was the same age as me. Louise is a pretty little creature, amusing, fascinating even. In addition, she's been well trained, if I may put it like that. In other words, she's assumed the habits of a certain set, a certain lifestyle.'

'I think I understand.'

'Then I don't need to be more specific. I'm not claiming that it's admirable, but it is human. The reporters don't understand that, and every time one of us has an affair, they say it's a great romance . . . Jean, my chequebook!'

He only had his dinner jacket left to put on. He looked at his watch.

'Last night, they had dinner out, then went to a night-club for a drink, I didn't ask which. As luck would have it, they ran into Marco in the company of a big blonde, a Dutch woman from the best society. They exchanged greetings from a distance, nothing more. Marco danced with his companion. Louise was on edge, and when she got back to the George-V with David, she told him, in the lift, that she felt like another bottle of champagne.'

'Does she drink a lot?'

'Too much. David also drank too much, but only in the evening. They chatted over their respective bottles – David only ever drank scotch – and I suspect that by the end the conversation was starting to become incoherent. After a few drinks, Louise tends to develop a guilt complex and accuses herself of every sin under the sun. What

I heard from her this lunchtime was that she told David she wasn't good enough for him, she despised herself for being nothing but a tortured female but couldn't stop herself from running after Marco and begging him to take her back.'

'How did Ward respond?'

'He didn't. He may not even have understood what she was saying. That's why I asked you if you had proof that someone held him under in the bath. Up until midnight, or one in the morning, he tended to hold out quite well, because he would only start drinking at five in the afternoon. By about two in the morning, he'd grow vague, and I often thought he might have an accident while taking a bath. I even advised him to always have a valet with him, but he hated feeling dependent on people. That's the reason he insisted on Arnold staying in another hotel. I wonder if it wasn't some kind of embarrassment on his part.

'That's pretty much it. Louise took off her clothes and put on a dressing gown. It's quite possible that, the bottle of champagne being empty, she took a swig of whisky. Then she got the idea into her head that she'd hurt David, and she wanted to go and apologize to him. Trust me, that's very much like her, I know her . . . She went along the corridor. She swore to me that she found the door ajar. She went in. In the bathroom, she saw what you already know and, instead of calling for help, she ran to her room and threw herself on her bed. According to her, she really did want to die, which is quite possible. So she took some sleeping pills. She was already using them when she was with me, especially when she'd been drinking.'

'How many pills?'

'I know what you're thinking, and you may be right. She wanted to die, because that would settle everything, but I don't suppose she would have been too upset to carry on living either. The intention was enough, it produced the same effect. The fact remains, she rang in time . . . Put yourself in her shoes. For her, all this was like a nightmare, one where the real and the unreal were so mixed up that she didn't know where she was.

'When she came round in the hospital, it was cold reality that prevailed. Her first thought was to phone Marco, and she called his number. There was no reply. So then she called a hotel in Rue de Ponthieu where he sometimes spends the night when he's in funds. He wasn't there either. That's when she thought of me. She didn't make much sense, but she did tell me that she was lost, that David was dead, that she herself had almost died, that she was sorry she hadn't, and she begged me to come running immediately. I told her it was impossible. After trying in vain to get more details from her, I advised her to go to Orly and take a plane for Nice.

'That's all, Maigret. I sent her to Lausanne, which she knows well, not in order to hide her from the police, but to avoid her being besieged by reporters and other snoopers, all the complications that are bound to ensue.

'You tell me that David was murdered, and I believe you. I can only state categorically that it wasn't Louise who killed him and that I haven't the slightest idea who did. Now . . .'

At last he put on his dinner jacket.

'If anyone asks for me, I'll be at the Sporting Club,' he said to his secretary.

'What shall I do if it's New York?'

'Tell them I've thought it over and the answer is no.'

'Very good, monsieur.'

'Are you coming, Maigret?'

They took the lift together, and when it reached the ground floor, they were unpleasantly surprised to get a photographer's flash full in their faces.

'I should have guessed,' Van Meulen muttered.

Shoving aside a podgy little man who was standing next to the photographer, trying to bar his way, he hurried to the exit.

'Detective Chief Inspector Maigret?'

The little man was a reporter from a local newspaper.

'Could I possibly talk to you for a moment?'

The porter was watching them from a distance and frowning.

'Maybe we could sit somewhere quiet . . .'

Maigret had enough experience of these situations to know that it was no use trying to get away, because then they would report him as saying things he had never said.

'I don't suppose I could buy you a drink at the bar?' the reporter continued.

'I've just had a drink.'

'With Joseph Van Meulen?'

'Yes.'

'Is it true that Countess Palmieri was on the Riviera this afternoon?'

'Yes, it is.'

Maigret had sat down in an enormous leather armchair, and the reporter was opposite him, perched on the edge of a chair, notepad in hand.

'I assume she's the prime suspect?'

'Why?'

'That's what they said when they phoned us from Paris.'

Someone must have alerted the press, either from the George-V or from the airport. Could one of the inspectors at Orly be in cahoots with a newspaper?

'Did you miss her?'

'By the time I got to Nice, she'd already left.'

'For Lausanne, I know.'

The press hadn't wasted any time.

'I just phoned the Lausanne Palace. She arrived there from Geneva by taxi. She seemed exhausted. She refused to answer any questions from the reporters who were waiting for her and went straight up to her suite, number 204.'

The man seemed pleased to be supplying all this gen to Detective Chief Inspector Maigret.

'She asked for a bottle of champagne to be brought up, then sent for a doctor, who's expected at any moment. Do you think she killed the colonel?'

'I'm not as quick as you and your colleagues.'

'Will you be going to Lausanne?'

'It's possible.'

'By tomorrow morning's plane? You do know that the

colonel's third wife lives in Lausanne and that she and Countess Palmieri can't stand each other?'

'No, I didn't know that.'

A strange interview, in which it was the reporter who was providing information.

'Assuming she's guilty, I don't suppose you're allowed to arrest her?'

'Not without an extradition warrant, no.'

'And I assume that in order to get an extradition warrant, it's necessary to supply positive proof?'

'Listen, my friend, I have the impression you're making up your article as you go along and I don't advise you to write it in that tone. There's no question of an arrest, or an extradition.'

'Isn't the countess a suspect?'

'I have no idea.'

'So—'

This time, Maigret lost his temper.

'No!' he almost yelled, even making the porter jump. 'I haven't told you anything for the perfectly good reason that I don't know anything, and if you put in my mouth the kind of suggestive statements you've just been spouting, you'll have me to answer to.'

'But—'

'No buts!' he said with finality, standing up and heading for the bar.

He was so angry that without even realizing it he ordered a Martini. The barman, who was looking at him curiously, must have recognized him from his photographs. Two or three people, sitting on high stools, turned and stared at him. In spite of the porter's precautions, everyone knew by now that he was in the hotel.

'Where are the phone booths?'

'On the left, in the corridor.'

Grumpily, he shut himself in the first one.

'Give me Paris, please. Danton 44.20.'

The lines weren't busy, and he only had five minutes to wait. He walked up and down the corridor. The telephone rang before the five minutes were up.

'Police Judiciaire? Put me through to the inspectors' office. This is Maigret . . . Hello? Is Lucas still there?'

He suspected that good old Lucas had also had an eventful day, and that he wouldn't be getting to bed early.

'Is that you, chief?'

'Yes. I'm in Monte Carlo. Any news?'

'You probably know by now that, despite all our precautions, the press has the story.'

'Yes, I know.'

'The third edition of *France-Soir* has a big article on its front page. At four in the afternoon, some English reporters arrived from London at the same time as a Monsieur Philps, some kind of lawyer or notary—'

'Solicitor.'

'That's it. He insisted on seeing the commissioner personally. They were together for more than an hour. When he came out, he was besieged by press people asking him questions and taking photographs of him, and he even hit one of the photographers with his umbrella and tried to smash his camera.'

'Is that all?'

'They're saying that Ward's mistress, the little countess, committed the murder, and that you personally are on her trail. Oh, and a man named John Arnold telephoned me. He seems furious.'

'What happened after that?'

'The reporters invaded the George-V. The hotel called the police to throw them out.'

'Where's Lapointe?'

'Right here. He'd like to talk to you. Shall I put him on?'

Lapointe's voice:

'Hello, chief? . . . I went to the American Hospital in Neuilly as agreed. I questioned the nurse, the switchboard operator and the receptionist. When she left, Countess Palmieri handed a letter to the receptionist and asked her to post it. It was addressed to Count Marco Palmieri in Rue de l'Étoile. As I hadn't learned anything interesting at the hospital, I went to that address. It's quite a smart-looking apartment house. I questioned the manageress, who was a bit reluctant to speak to me at first. Apparently, Count Palmieri didn't sleep there last night, which isn't unusual for him. He came back about eleven o'clock this morning, looking worried, without even dropping by the lodge to see if there was any mail for him. Less than half an hour later, he set off again, carrying a little suitcase. There's been no sign of him since.'

Maigret was silent, because he had nothing to say, and he sensed that at the other end Lapointe was disconcerted.

'What do I do? Should I keep looking for him?'

'If you like.'

The reply was ideally phrased to disorientate Lapointe even more.

'Don't you think . . . ?'

What had Van Meulen told him earlier? Everyone was capable of committing murder, provided there was sufficient motive. Passion . . . Could that be the case here, when Louise had been married for nearly three years to another man and had been the colonel's mistress for more than a year? Hadn't she actually been on the verge of leaving the colonel and going back to her first husband?

Financial gain? How would Palmieri benefit from Ward's death?

Maigret was somewhat discouraged, as often happened to him at the beginning of an investigation. There was always a moment when the people involved seemed unreal and there was something insubstantial about their actions.

During such periods, Maigret was sullen, somehow heavier, denser than usual. Even though young Lapointe was the newest in the team, he was starting to know him well enough to realize what was happening, even at the other end of a telephone line.

'I'll do my best, chief. I've drawn up a list of the people who are in those photographs. There are just two or three still to be identified.'

The air was stifling in the booth, especially as Maigret wasn't dressed for the Riviera. He went back to the bar to finish his drink and noticed tables laid for dinner on the terrace.

'Can I eat here?'

'Yes. But I think those tables are reserved, as they are every evening. We can seat you inside.'

Good God! If they'd dared, they would probably have asked him to eat with the staff!

5.

In which Maigret finally meets somebody who doesn't have money and worries about it

He slept badly, without completely losing consciousness of the place where he was, the hotel with its 200 open windows, the street lamps around the public gardens with their bluish lawns, the casino as faded in its charms as the old ladies in their old-fashioned outfits whom he had seen entering after dinner, the lazy sea which, every twelve seconds – he had counted them over and over, the way others count sheep – fell in a wet fringe on the rocky shore.

Cars stopped outside and left again, performing complicated manoeuvres. Their doors slammed. Voices were so distinct that you felt you were being indiscreet, and there were still noisy coaches bringing in gamblers in batches and taking others away. There was music, too, on the terrace of the Café de Paris opposite.

When, by some miracle, silence briefly fell, the light, anachronistic sound of a horse-drawn carriage could be discerned in the background, like a flute in an orchestra.

He had left his window open because he was hot. But

as he hadn't brought any luggage with him and was lying there without pyjamas, he was soon freezing cold and went to close the window. As he did so, he glanced sullenly at the lights of the Sporting Club over at the far end of the beach, where Joseph Van Meulen, 'Daddy', as the little countess called him, was presiding over a table of twenty people.

Because his mood was no longer the same, these people appeared to him in a different light, and he was angry with himself now, felt almost humiliated at having listened to Van Meulen like a well-behaved child, almost without daring to interrupt him.

Had he been flattered, when it came down to it, that such a respectable man should treat him with such friendly familiarity? Unlike John T. Arnold, the plump, annoyingly self-confident little Englishman, Van Meulen hadn't seemed to be giving him a lecture on the habits of a certain social set and had even appeared touched by the fact that Maigret had come all that way in person.

'Now, you,' he seemed to be saying constantly, 'you understand me.'

Had Maigret allowed himself to be taken in? *Daddy . . . The little countess . . . David . . .* And all these other first names they used without bothering to specify who they were talking about, as if the whole world simply had to be in the know . . .

He dozed off a little, turned over heavily, suddenly had an image of the colonel naked in his bath, then of Van Meulen, also naked, being kneaded by the masseur who looked like a boxer.

Were these people too civilized to be above suspicion?

'Any man is capable of committing murder, provided he has sufficient motive and is convinced he won't get caught.'

Van Meulen, though, didn't think that passion was sufficient motive. Hadn't he been subtly implying that for some people, passion is almost unthinkable?

'At our age . . . A pleasant young woman, who's been well trained . . .'

Their *little countess* had called the doctor, had moaned and groaned, had let herself be taken to hospital, then quietly telephoned, first to Paris, trying to reach her first husband who was still her occasional lover, then good old *Daddy* Van Meulen.

She knew that Ward was dead. She had seen the body. The poor little thing was at her wits' end.

Should she call the police? Out of the question. She was far too shaken. And what could the police, with their big boots and their narrow minds, understand of the affairs of people like *them*?

'Get on a plane, my dear. Come and see me and I'll advise you.'

Meanwhile, the other man, John T. Arnold, arrived at the George-V and handed out advice, made barely veiled suggestions.

'Please don't tell the press. Handle with care. This business is dynamite. There are major interests at stake. The whole world will be shaken.'

And yet he was the one who had phoned the lawyers in London and told them to come running, probably to help him cover things up.

Van Meulen, as calmly as if it was the most natural, most legitimate thing in the world, had sent Countess Palmieri to Lausanne to rest.

No, she wasn't running away. She wasn't trying to evade the police.

'You see, she's used to the place. She'll avoid being besieged by reporters and all the other fuss that surrounds a police investigation.'

It was up to Maigret to make a move again, to take another plane . . .

Maigret hated over-simplification. His judgements of people didn't depend on how much money they had, or didn't have. He was determined to keep a cool head, but there were a hundred things he couldn't help being irritated by.

He heard people who had come back from the famous gala dinner talking loudly outside, then in their suites, opening taps, flushing toilets.

He was the first person up, at six in the morning, and he shaved with the cheap razor he'd had a bellboy buy him along with a toothbrush. It took him nearly half an hour to get a cup of coffee. The lobby was being cleaned when he crossed it. When he asked the worn-looking receptionist for his bill, the man replied:

'Monsieur Van Meulen left instructions—'

'It's not up to Monsieur Van Meulen to give instructions.'

He insisted on paying. Outside the door, the Belgian's Rolls was waiting, the chauffeur holding the door open.

'Monsieur Van Meulen has asked me to drive you to the airport.'

He decided to get in anyway, because he had never ridden in a Rolls-Royce. He was early. He bought some newspapers. On its front page, the Nice paper carried a photograph of him and Van Meulen coming out of the lift, with the caption: *Detective Chief Inspector Maigret leaving a meeting with the billionaire Van Meulen.*

A meeting!

The Paris newspapers carried the headline:

ENGLISH BILLIONAIRE FOUND DEAD IN HIS BATH

The word 'billionaire' was repeated a lot.

Murder or accident?

The reporters probably weren't up yet, and he was left in peace to board his plane. He fastened his seat belt and looked absently through the window as the sea grew distant and little white houses with red roofs appeared, strewn over the dark green of the mountains.

'Coffee or tea?'

He seemed to be brooding. When the stewardess insisted, he didn't even grant her a smile. When, under a cloudless sky, he discovered the Alps beneath him, with great streaks of snow, he wouldn't even admit that it was a magnificent sight.

Less than ten minutes later they entered a small area of mist that ran alongside the plane and soon metamorphosed into opaque steam, like the kind you see emerging from locomotives as they pull into stations with their whistles blowing.

In Geneva, it was raining. The rain hadn't only just started. It was obvious that it had been raining for a long time: it was cold, and everyone was wearing coats.

No sooner had he put his foot on the gangway than the flashes went off. There may not have been any reporters when he left, but they were waiting for him when he arrived, seven or eight of them, with their notebooks and their questions.

'I have nothing to say.'

'Will you be going to Lausanne?'

'I have no idea.'

He brushed them aside, helped, most considerately, by a Swissair representative who, sparing him the formalities and the queues, shepherded him through the non-public areas of the airport.

'Do you have a car? Are you taking the train to Lausanne?'

'I think I'll take a taxi.'

'I'll call you one.'

Two cars followed his, filled with reporters and photographers. Still surly, he tried to doze in a corner, glancing vaguely from time to time at the wet vines and the patches of grey lake glimpsed between the trees.

What annoyed him the most was the impression he had that whatever he was doing had been decided for him. He wasn't going to Lausanne because it was his idea to go there, but because a path had been marked out for him that led there, whether he liked it or not.

His taxi came to a halt by the columns outside the Lausanne Palace. The photographers mobbed him. He was asked questions. The doorman helped him to force his way through.

Inside, he encountered the same atmosphere as at the George-V or the Hôtel de Paris, as if people who travelled were determined not to change scenery. It was perhaps a little heavier, more solemn here, with a porter in a black frock coat discreetly embellished with gold. He spoke five or six languages, like the others, and the only difference was that in French he had a slight Germanic accent.

'Is Countess Palmieri here?'

'Yes, inspector. In suite 204 as usual.'

An Asian family sat in armchairs in the lobby, waiting for something or other. The wife wore a gold sari, and her three children looked at him with curiosity in their big brown eyes.

It was barely ten in the morning.

'I don't suppose she's up yet?'

'She rang for her breakfast half an hour ago. Would you like me to inform her that you're here? I think she's expecting you.'

'Do you know if she's made or received any telephone calls?'

'You'd have to ask the operator. Hans, take the chief inspector to the switchboard.'

It was in a room at the end of a corridor behind reception, where three women sat side by side.

'Could you tell me—'

'One moment.' Then, in English: 'You're through to Bangkok, monsieur.'

'Could you tell me if Countess Palmieri has made or received any telephone calls since she arrived?'

They had lists in front of them.

'Last night, at one o'clock, she received a call from Monte Carlo.'

Probably Van Meulen, *Daddy*, taking the trouble between dances at the Sporting Club, or more likely between two card games, to find out how she was.

'This morning she called Paris.'

'What number?'

It was the number of Marco's bachelor apartment in Rue de l'Étoile.

'Was there any answer?'

'No. She left a message asking to be called back.'

'Was that the only one?'

'About ten minutes ago, she asked for Monte Carlo again.'

'Did she get through?'

'Yes, twice. Three minutes each time.'

'Could you announce me?'

'Gladly, Monsieur Maigret.'

It was stupid. Having heard so much about her, he was somewhat overawed, which he found humiliating. Going up in the lift, he felt almost like a young man going to see a famous actress in the flesh for the first time.

'This way.'

The bellboy knocked at a door. A voice answered, 'Come in.' The door was opened for him, and Maigret found himself in a sitting room with a view of the lake through its two windows.

There was nobody here. A voice reached him from the bedroom, the door to which was ajar.

'Take a seat, inspector. I'll be right with you.'

On a tray, bacon and eggs that had hardly been touched, a few rolls and a crumbled croissant. He thought he caught the characteristic sound of a bottle being closed. At last, a swish of silk.

'Please forgive me . . .'

Again like the man who surprises an actress in an intimate moment, he was disconcerted, disappointed. Before him stood a very nondescript little woman, barely made up, pale-faced, with tired eyes, holding out a moist, trembling hand.

'Please sit down.'

Through the half-open door, he glimpsed an unmade bed, things left lying around, a bottle of pills on the night table.

She sat down facing him and folded over her legs the ends of a cream silk dressing gown transparent enough to let her nightdress show through.

'I'm so sorry to have put you to all this trouble.'

She looked every one of her thirty-nine years. In fact, right now she looked even older. There were deep blue shadows under her eyes and thin lines at the corner of each nostril.

She wasn't pretending to be tired. She was genuinely weary, at the end of her tether. He would have sworn that she was ready to burst into tears at any moment. She was looking at him, unsure what to say, when the telephone rang.

'Do you mind?'

'Please go ahead.'

'Hello? . . . Yes, speaking . . . Put her through . . . Hello, Anne . . . It's kind of you to call me . . . Thank you . . . Yes . . . Yes . . . I don't know yet . . . I have someone with me at the moment . . . No, don't ask me to come out . . . Yes . . . Tell His Highness . . . Thank you . . . Speak to you soon . . .'

There were tiny beads of sweat on her upper lip, and as she spoke, Maigret could smell alcohol on her breath.

'Are you very angry with me?'

She wasn't putting on an act. She seemed quite natural, too shaken to be capable of playing a role.

'It's so awful, so unexpected! And the very day when—'

'When you were going to tell Colonel Ward that you'd made up your mind to leave him? Is that what you meant?'

She nodded.

'I think Jef – I think Van Meulen has told you everything, hasn't he? I'm wondering what else I could tell you. Are you going to take me back to Paris?'

'Does that worry you?'

'I don't know. He advised me to go with you if that was what you decided. I'm doing everything he told me. He's such an intelligent man, so good, so superior! It's as if he knows everything, can predict everything.'

'He didn't predict the death of his friend Ward.'

'But he did predict that I would get back together with Marco.'

'Was that already arranged between Marco and you? I thought when you ran into him in the nightclub, your first husband was with a young Dutch woman, and you didn't even speak to him.'

'That's true. All the same, I decided . . .'

Her nervous hands, older than her face, couldn't keep still. Her fingers intertwined, leaving white marks on her knuckles.

'How can I explain this to you, when I don't know myself? Everything was going well. I thought I was over it. David and I were waiting for the last papers to be signed so that we could get married. David was a man like Van Meulen, not exactly the same, but almost.'

'What do you mean by that?'

'With *Daddy*, I have the impression he always tells me what he thinks. Not necessarily everything, because he doesn't want to tire me with details, but I feel there's a real connection, if you know what I mean . . . David, on the other hand, would watch me with those big eyes of his, always with an amused little gleam in them. Maybe it wasn't me he was laughing at, but himself. He was like a big cat, very crafty, very philosophical . . .'

She repeated:

'If you know what I mean.'

'At the beginning of the evening, when you went to dinner with the colonel, were you already intending to break it off with him?'

She thought about this for a moment.

'No.'

Then she corrected herself:

'But I suspected it would happen one day.'

'Why?'

'Because it wasn't the first time. Not that I wanted to get back with Marco, because I knew perfectly well . . .'

She bit her lip.

'What did you know?'

'That it would mean starting all over again. He doesn't have any money, and neither do I.'

She was suddenly off on a new track, speaking in the rapid, staccato fashion of a drug addict.

'I don't have any money, you know. I don't own a single thing. If Van Meulen hadn't transferred money to my bank that morning, the cheque I signed at the airport would have bounced. He had to give me some more yesterday so that I could come here. I'm very poor.'

'Your jewellery . . .'

'Jewellery, yes. And my mink. That's all!'

'But the colonel . . . ?'

She sighed, despairing of getting across what she meant.

'It's not the way you think. He paid for my apartment, my travels, he paid my bills. But I never had any money in my bag. As long as I was with him I didn't need any.'

'Whereas once you were married . . .'

'It would have been the same.'

'He made sure his other three wives had an income.'

'Afterwards! Once he'd left them.'

He came straight out with it:

'Was he doing this to stop you giving money to Marco?'

She stared at him.

'I don't think so. I never thought about it. David never had any money in his pockets either. It was Arnold who paid the bills at the end of the month. Now, I'm forty years old and . . .'

She looked around her as if to say that she was going to have to leave all this. The yellowish furrows at the sides of her nose grew deeper. Hesitantly, she got to her feet.

'Will you excuse me for a moment?'

She hurried into the bedroom and closed the door behind her, and when she returned, Maigret again smelled alcohol on her breath.

'What did you just drink?'

'A slug of whisky, if you must know. I'm ready to drop. Sometimes I can go for weeks without drinking.'

'Except champagne?'

'A glass of champagne from time to time, yes. But when I'm in the state I'm in now, I need . . .'

He would have sworn that she had drunk straight from the bottle, greedily, in the way some drug addicts inject themselves through their clothes in order not to waste time.

Her eyes were shinier, her delivery more voluble.

'I swear I hadn't made up my mind. I saw Marco with that woman, and it gave me a shock.'

'Did you know her?'

'Yes. She's a divorcee, and her husband, who's in shipping, had business dealings with David.'

These men knew each other, met around board tables,

on beaches, in nightclubs, and apparently the same women went quite naturally from one man's bed to another's.

'I knew that Marco and she had had an affair in Deauville. I'd even been told that she'd decided to marry him, but I didn't believe it. She's very rich, and he has nothing.'

'So you got it into your head to prevent the marriage?'

Her lips had grown thinner and harder.

'Yes.'

'Do you think Marco would have let you?'

Her eyes were watering, but she refused to cry.

'I don't know. I wasn't thinking. I kept watching them. He deliberately passed straight by me as he danced, without so much as a glance at me.'

'So, logically, it's Marco who should have been killed?'

'What do you mean?'

'Didn't you ever think of killing him? Didn't you threaten him at any time?'

'How do you know that?'

'Didn't he think you capable of it?'

'Van Meulen told you, didn't he?'

'No.'

'It isn't as simple as that. We'd been drinking over dinner. At the Monseigneur, I had a whole bottle of champagne and I think I also had a few sips from David's glass of whisky. I was considering making a scene, going and tearing Marco from the arms of that horrible fat woman with her pink baby skin. David insisted that we leave, so in the end I went with him. In the taxi, I didn't say a word. I was planning to leave the hotel later and go back to the nightclub to . . . I don't know why. Don't ask me to explain. David must have sensed it. He was the one who suggested we have a last drink in my suite.'

'Why in yours?'

The question took her aback and she echoed:

'Why?'

It was as if she, too, were looking for the answer.

'David always came to my suite. I don't think he liked . . . He was quite protective of his privacy.'

'Did you tell him you were planning to leave him?'

'I told him everything I'd been thinking, that I was just a bitch, that I'd never be happy without Marco, that Marco simply had to put in an appearance and I . . .'

'What was his response?'

'He kept calmly drinking his whisky, looking at me with his big sad eyes. "What about the money?" he said in the end. "You know perfectly well that Marco . . ."'

'Was he right about Marco?'

'Marco has big needs.'

'Hasn't it ever occurred to him to get a job?'

She stared at him in amazement, as if the question revealed boundless naivety.

'What would he do? . . . In the end, I got undressed.'

'Did anything happen between David and you?'

Another surprised look.

'Nothing ever happened. You don't understand . . . David had also drunk a lot, as he did every night before going to bed.'

'A third of a bottle?'

'Not completely. I know why you're asking me that. But

I was the one who had a little whisky when he left, because I didn't feel well. All I wanted was to collapse on the bed and not have to think any more. I tried to sleep. Then I told myself that it wouldn't work with Marco, that it would never work, and that the best thing I could do was die.'

'How many pills did you take?'

'I don't know. As many as I could hold in the palm of my hand. I felt better. I was crying softly, and starting to fall asleep. Then I imagined my funeral, the cemetery, the . . . I started to struggle. I was scared that it was too late, that I wouldn't be able to call anyone. I was already too weak to cry out. The buttons you press to ring for people seemed a long way away. My arm was heavy. It was like one of those dreams when you try to run away and your legs refuse to carry you. But I must have reached the bell, because someone came . . .'

She broke off on seeing the suddenly cold, hard expression on Maigret's face.

'Why are you looking at me like that?'

'Why are you lying?'

He had almost let himself be taken in.

'At what point did you go to the colonel's room?'

'That's true. I'd forgotten . . .'

'You'd forgotten that you went there?'

She shook her head and at last started crying.

'Please don't be hard on me. I swear I didn't mean to lie to you. The proof of that is that I told Jef Van Meulen the truth. Only, when I found myself in the hospital and started to panic, my first thought was to claim that I didn't know what had happened. I was sure they wouldn't believe me, that they'd suspect me of killing David. So, just now, talking to you, I forgot that Van Meulen advised me not to hide anything.'

'How long after the colonel left did you go to his suite?'

'Will you believe me this time?'

'That depends.'

'You see! It's always the same thing with me. I do what I can. I have nothing to hide. Only, my head starts spinning, and I get all confused. Will you allow me to go and take a sip, just a sip? I promise I won't get drunk. I can't stand it any more, inspector!'

He let her and almost felt like asking her for a drink for himself.

'It was before I took the pills. I hadn't yet made up my mind to die, but I'd already had the whisky. I was drunk and sick. I regretted what I'd said to David. Suddenly, life terrified me. I saw myself old and alone, without money, unable to earn a living, because I've never known how to do anything. David was my last chance. When I left Van Meulen, I was younger. The proof of that is—'

'That you then found the colonel.'

She seemed surprised, hurt by his aggressiveness.

'Think whatever you like about me. At least I know you're wrong . . . I was afraid that David would leave me. I went to his suite in my nightdress, I didn't even put on a dressing gown, and I found the door ajar.'

'I asked you how long it had been since he'd left you.'

'I don't know. I remember I smoked several cigarettes.

You must have seen them in the ashtray. David only smoked cigars.'

'Did you see anyone in his suite?'

'Only him. I almost screamed. I'm not sure I didn't.'

'Was he dead?'

She looked at him, eyes wide open, as if the idea had never occurred to her before.

'I think so. At least I thought so at the time, and I ran out.'

'Did you pass anyone in the corridor?'

'No . . . Oh, wait! I heard the lift coming up. I'm sure of that, because I started running.'

'Did you drink some more?'

'Maybe, without thinking. Then I felt so down that I took the pills. The rest I've already told you. Could I . . . ?'

No doubt she was going to ask permission to take another swig of whisky, but just then the telephone rang, and she reached out an unsteady arm.

'Hello? . . . Yes, he's here.'

It was soothing, almost refreshing, to hear Lucas' calm voice, a normal voice at last, and to imagine him sitting at his desk at Quai des Orfèvres.

'Is that you, chief?'

'I was going to call you later.'

'I assumed you might, but I thought it best to let you know right away. Marco Palmieri is here.'

'You found him?'

'We didn't exactly find him. He came of his own free will. He arrived about twenty minutes ago, fresh as a daisy, very casual. He asked if you were here and when he was told you weren't, he asked to speak to one of your colleagues. They sent him to me. For the moment, I've left him in your office with Janvier.'

'What is he saying?'

'That he didn't know about any of this until he read about it in the papers.'

'Last night?'

'No, not until this morning. He wasn't in Paris, but with friends who have a chateau in the Nièvre and were holding a hunting party.'

'Was the Dutch woman with him?'

'At the hunting party? Yes. They left together in her car. He tells me they're getting married. Her name is Anna de Groot, and she's divorced.'

'I know. Go on.'

Slumped in her armchair, the little countess was listening to him and biting her nails, from which the polish was flaking off.

'I asked him to account for his whereabouts the previous night.'

'And?'

'He was in a nightclub, the Monseigneur.'

'I know.'

'With Anna de Groot.'

'I know that, too.'

'He spotted the colonel with his ex-wife.'

'And then?'

'He saw the Dutch woman home.'

'Where's that?'

'The George-V. She has a suite on the fourth floor.'

'What time was that?'

'According to him, about three thirty, maybe four. I sent someone to check, but I haven't heard yet. They went to bed, and he didn't get up until ten in the morning. He claims that they were invited to this hunting party at the chateau of a banker from Rue Auber more than a week ago. Marco Palmieri left the George-V and went to his place by taxi to pick up his suitcase. He kept the taxi, which parked outside the door. He went back to the George-V, and at about half past eleven the couple set off in Anna de Groot's Jaguar. This morning, just as they were about to go out hunting, he skimmed through the newspapers in the entrance hall of the chateau. He came straight back to Paris, still with his boots on.'

'Did the Dutch woman come with him?'

'She stayed there. Lapointe phoned the chateau to check, and a butler told him she was at the hunt.'

'What's your impression of him?'

'He's very much at ease. He seems genuine. He's really quite a nice young man.'

Oh, yes, they were all so nice!

'What should I do with him?'

'Send Lapointe to the George-V. I'd like him to establish exactly who came and went that night. Get him to question the night staff.'

'He'll have to go to their homes. They're not on duty during the day.'

'Have him do that. As for . . .'

He preferred not to say the name out loud in front of Countess Palmieri, who hadn't taken her eyes off him.

'As for your visitor, given the stage we're at right now,

the only thing you can do is let him go. Advise him not to leave Paris. Get someone to . . . That's right, the usual procedure . . . I'll call you back later. I'm not alone.'

For some reason, he asked at the last moment:

'What's the weather like there?'

'Chilly, with a bit of harsh sunshine.'

As he hung up, the little countess asked:

'Is it him?'

'Who?'

'Marco. It's him you were talking about, isn't it?'

'Are you sure you didn't see him in the corridors of the George-V or in the colonel's suite?'

She leaped from her armchair, so overexcited that he was afraid she was having a nervous breakdown.

'I thought as much!' she cried, her face distorted. 'He was there with her, wasn't he, right above my head? Oh, yes, I know! She always stays at the George-V. I made inquiries about which suite she was in. They were both there, in bed.'

She seemed wild with anger.

'They were there, laughing, making love, while I—'

'Don't you think rather that Marco was—'

'Was what?'

'Perhaps holding the colonel's head underwater?'

She couldn't believe her ears. Her body swayed beneath her transparent dressing gown, and suddenly she threw herself at Maigret, hitting out wildly with her clenched fists.

'Are you mad? Are you mad? How dare you? You're a monster! You . . .'

He felt ridiculous, stuck here in a hotel suite, trying to grab a fury by the wrists while her anger increased her energy tenfold.

His tie askew, his hair dishevelled, gasping for breath, he was finally managing to immobilize her when there was a knock at the door.

6.

*In which Maigret is invited to lunch, and in which the talk is
still of VIPs*

It had ended less badly than Maigret might have feared.
For the little countess, those knocks at the door were
providential, because they allowed her to get out of a
scene she probably didn't know how to end.

Once again, she had rushed into the bedroom, while
Maigret, unhurriedly arranging his tie and smoothing his
hair, went and opened the door to the corridor.

It was quite simply the floor waiter, looking suddenly
intimidated and asking if he could take away the breakfast
tray. Had he been listening at the door, or had he, without
specifically listening, caught the echoes of the scene? If
so, he didn't show it, and when he left, the countess re-
appeared, calmer now, wiping her lips.

'I assume you're planning to take me back to Paris?'

'Even if I wanted to, I'd have to go through some pretty
lengthy formalities.'

'My lawyer here wouldn't let you obtain extradition.
But I want to go, I'm determined to attend David's funeral.
Are you taking the four o'clock plane?'

'Quite likely, but you're not taking it.'

'And why is that, may I ask?'

'Because I don't want to travel with you.'

'It's my right, isn't it?'

Maigret was thinking of the reporters and photographers who would be sure to mob her, both in Geneva and at Orly.

'It may be your right, but if you try to take that plane, I'll find a more or less legal way to stop you. I don't suppose you have any statement to make to me?'

When all was said and done, this interview had ended in an almost grotesque fashion, and to recover his footing in a familiar reality, Maigret had next had a telephone conversation of nearly half an hour with Lucas. The hotel management had spontaneously offered him a little office near reception.

Although Doctor Paul hadn't yet sent in his official report, he had given Lucas a preliminary report over the phone. After the post-mortem, he was more than ever convinced that someone had held David Ward down in his bath, since there was no other way to explain the bruises on his shoulders. In addition, there was no trauma to the neck or back, as there almost certainly would have been if the colonel had slipped, hit the edge of the bath and knocked himself unconscious.

Janvier had been tailing Marco. As was to be expected, the first concern of the little countess's ex-husband, on leaving Quai des Orfèvres, had been to phone Anna de Groot.

Lucas was overwhelmed by telephone calls, many from large banks and financial companies.

'Will you be back this afternoon, chief?'

'I'm taking the four o'clock plane.'

As he put the telephone down, he was handed an envelope which a uniformed police officer had just brought for him. It was a charming note from the director of the Sûreté in Lausanne, saying that he would be delighted to have the opportunity to at last meet the famous Maigret and inviting him to 'a very simple lunch, by the lake, in a quiet Vaudois inn'.

Maigret, who had half an hour to kill, telephoned Boulevard Richard-Lenoir.

'Are you still in Lausanne?' Madame Maigret asked.

Headquarters had informed her the previous day of her husband's departure, and she had also read about it in the morning newspapers.

'I'll be taking the plane this afternoon, but that doesn't mean I'll be home early. Don't wait for me for dinner.'

'Are you bringing the countess back with you?'

It wasn't jealousy, of course, but for the first time Maigret seemed to sense an anxiety, as well as a barely perceptible hint of irony, in his wife's voice.

'I have no desire to bring her back.'

'Oh!'

He lit his pipe and left the hotel, announcing to the porter that if anyone asked for him, he would be back in a few minutes. Two photographers followed him, hoping that he was about to do something revealing.

His hands in his pockets, he contented himself with looking in the shop windows and going into a tobacconist's to buy a pipe, because he had left in such a rush that, unusually, he only had one in his pocket.

He let himself be tempted by the tins of tobaccos unknown in France, took three different kinds, then, as if overcome with remorse, went into the shop next door and bought a handkerchief embroidered with the arms of Lausanne for Madame Maigret.

The director of the Sûreté came to pick him up at the appointed time. He was a big, strapping man with an athletic physique, probably an enthusiastic skier.

'Do you mind if we go and eat in the country, a few kilometres from here? Don't worry about your plane. I'll have you driven to the airport in one of our cars.'

He had a fair complexion, and his cheeks were so closely shaven that they gleamed. His appearance and manner were those of a man who has kept in close touch with the countryside, and indeed Maigret was to learn that his father was a vineyard owner near Vevey.

They settled down in an inn by the lake, where, besides them, there was only one table, full of local people who were talking about the choir they belonged to.

'Will you allow me to choose the menu?'

He ordered dried meat – rustic ham and sausage – from Grisons, followed by a freshwater fish, an Arctic char.

He was looking at Maigret with discreet, furtive little glances that betrayed his curiosity and his admiration.

'She's a strange woman, isn't she?'

'The countess?'

'Yes. We know her well. She spends part of the year in Lausanne.'

He explained, not without a certain touching pride:

'We're a small country, Monsieur Maigret. But, precisely

because we're a small country, the proportion of VIPs is greater here than in Paris or even on the Riviera. You may have more of them than us, but with you they're rather lost in the crowd. Here, there's no way not to see them. And of course they're the same people you find on the Champs-Élysées or the Croisette.'

Maigret did justice to the food and the local white wine, which had been served chilled in a misted carafe.

'We're familiar with Colonel Ward, and with pretty much all the people you're dealing with right now. By the way, Ward's third wife, Muriel, left for Paris in a hurry this morning.'

'What kind of life does she lead in Lausanne?'

The director had blue eyes which, when he stopped to think, became clearer, almost transparent.

'It isn't easy to explain. She has a comfortable, almost luxurious, though rather small apartment in a new block in Ouchy. Her daughter Ellen is a boarder in a school attended mainly by American, English, Dutch and German girls from good families. We have a lot of schools like that in Switzerland, and children are sent here from around the world.'

'I know.'

'Muriel Ward – I say Ward, because the divorce hasn't yet been finalized, and she still uses the name – belongs to what we call the single women's club. It isn't a real club, of course. There are no rules, no membership cards, no fees. It's what we call the women who come to Switzerland to live on their own, for various reasons. Some are divorced, others widows. There are also a few opera singers and musicians, and some women whom their husbands still visit now and again. The reasons they have for being here are their own business, aren't they? Sometimes it's political, sometimes financial, it may even be for health reasons. There are members of royal families and untitled people, wealthy widows and women who have only modest incomes.'

He said all this rather like a guide, with a slight smile, which tinged his words with humour.

'All of them, whether because of their names, their fortunes, or for some other reason, are considered important people – VIPs, as I said. And they form groups. Not a club. A series of groups who are more or less friends or enemies. Some live all year round at the Lausanne Palace, which you've seen. The richest have villas in Ouchy, or chateaux in the surrounding area. They invite each other to tea, or meet at concerts . . . But isn't it the same in Paris? The difference, as I said before, is that here they're more conspicuous. We have men, too, who come from all over, and who've decided to live all year or part of the year in Switzerland. For example, talking again of the Lausanne Palace, there are currently about twenty people there from the family of King Saud. Add the delegates to international conferences, UNESCO and others, which take place in our country, and you'll understand that we have our work cut out. I think our police, although discreet, are quite efficient, so if I can be of any use to you . . .'

Maigret had gradually assumed the same smile as the director. He understood that while Swiss hospitality was generous, the police were nevertheless very well informed about the actions of all these celebrities.

What he had just been told amounted to:

'If you have any questions to ask . . .'

He murmured:

'It seems that Ward got on perfectly well with his ex-wives . . .'

'Why should he bear them any grudges? He was the one who left them when he'd had enough of them.'

'Was he generous?'

'Not excessively. He gave them enough to live with dignity, but it wasn't a fortune.'

'What kind of woman is Muriel Halligan?'

'An American.'

In his mouth, that word took on great meaning.

'I don't know why the colonel chose to ask for a divorce in Switzerland. Unless he had other reasons for settling here. Whatever the reason, the proceedings have been dragging on for two years. Muriel chose the two best lawyers in the country, which must be costing her plenty. She upholds the idea, admitted apparently by some American courts, that once a husband has accustomed his wife to a certain lifestyle, he has to ensure she can keep the same lifestyle to the end of her days.'

'And the colonel wouldn't agree to that?'

'He has excellent lawyers, too. Three or four times it was rumoured that they'd come to an agreement, but I don't think the final papers were ever signed.'

'I assume that while the proceedings continue, the wife tries to avoid having flings?'

The director refilled the glasses with deliberate slowness, as if determined to weigh his words.

'Flings, no. These ladies in the club generally keep their love lives discreet . . . You've met John T. Arnold, I assume?'

'He was the first to come running to the George-V.'

'He's a bachelor,' was the laconic reply.

'And . . . ?'

'For a while, it was rumoured that he was somewhat differently inclined. But as I happen to know through the staff of the hotels where he stays, that isn't the case.'

'What else do you know?'

'He was very close to the colonel and had been for a very long time. He was his confidant, his secretary, his business associate. Aside from his legal marriages, the colonel always had his little flings, most of them short, often no more than a night or even an hour. As he was too lazy to court women himself, and as, in his situation, he found it tricky to proposition a nightclub dancer, for example, or a flower-seller, John T. Arnold would take care of it for him.'

'I see.'

'Then you can guess the rest. Arnold took his commission in kind. It's claimed, although I have no actual evidence, that he took his commission with Ward's wives, too.'

'Including Muriel?'

'He's been to Lausanne twice on his own to see her. But there's nothing to prove he wasn't on an errand for Ward.'

'What about the countess?'

'Definitely! And not only Arnold in her case. When she's

drunk enough champagne, she often needs a shoulder to cry on.'

'Did Ward know?'

'I never had much to do with Colonel Ward. Don't forget I'm only a policeman.'

They both smiled. It was a curious conversation, in which not everything was openly expressed, a conversation full of innuendo.

'In my opinion, Ward knew a lot of things, but wasn't particularly affected by them. I learned from this morning's newspapers that in Monte Carlo you met Monsieur Van Meulen, who's another of our guests. They were great friends, both men who've lived a lot, and neither of them ever asked of people, women in particular, more than they could give. They're very much of the same calibre, except that Van Meulen is cooler and more self-controlled, whereas the colonel was a bit of a drinker . . . I assume you'll have coffee?'

Maigret was to keep for a long time the memory of lunch in this little restaurant, which reminded him of an open-air tavern on the banks of the Marne, but with a touch of Swiss seriousness, less zest, perhaps, and more genuine intimacy.

'Is the countess taking the same plane as you?'

'I forbade her to do so.'

'That'll depend on what she drinks between now and four o'clock. You'd prefer her not to take it?'

'She's quite conspicuous, and something of a nuisance.'

'She won't take it,' the director promised. 'Would it bother you too much if I asked you to pay a short visit to our offices? My men would so much like to meet you . . .'

He was shown around the premises of the Sûreté, which were in a brand-new building, on the same floor as a private bank and just below a ladies' hairdresser. Maigret shook hands, smiled and repeated the same kind words ten times. The local white wine he had drunk filled him with a sense of well-being.

'Now it's time I put you in a car. If you're late, we'll be forced to sound the siren all the way . . .'

Soon he was back in the atmosphere of airports, the loudspeaker announcements, the bars with uniformed pilots and stewardesses hastily drinking their coffees.

Then came the plane, mountains higher than those this morning, meadows and farms glimpsed between clouds.

Lapointe was waiting for him at Orly with one of the Police Judiciaire's black cars.

'Did you have a good trip, chief?'

Here again were the suburbs, then Paris on a fine late afternoon.

'Hasn't it been raining?'

'Not a drop. I thought it was best to come and get you.'

'Anything new?'

'I'm not up to date with everything. All the information comes in to Lucas. I went to see some of the night staff, which meant quite a bit of travelling, because most of these people live in the suburbs.'

'What did you find out?'

'Nothing specific. I tried to establish a timetable of when everyone went in and out. It wasn't easy. Apparently there are 310 guests at the hotel, everyone comes and goes, makes phone calls, rings for the waiter or the chambermaid, calls for a taxi, a bellboy, a manicurist, whatever. Plus, the staff are afraid to say too much. Most of them answer evasively.'

Still driving, he took a paper from his pocket and passed it to Maigret.

8 p.m. The third floor chambermaid enters 332, the countess's suite, and finds the countess in her dressing gown, receiving a manicure.

'Is it for the blanket, Annette?'

'Yes, countess.'

'Would you mind coming back in half an hour?'

8.10. Colonel Ward is in the bar of the hotel with John T. Arnold. The colonel looks at his watch, leaves his companion and goes up to his suite. Arnold orders a sandwich.

8.22. From his suite, the colonel asks for a call to Cambridge and speaks to his son. Apparently he made similar calls twice a week, always about the same time.

About 8.30. In the bar, Arnold goes into the phone booth. He must have made a call within Paris, because the switchboard operator has no record of it.

8.45. From 347, the colonel phones 332, probably to find out if the countess is ready.

About 9.00. The colonel and the countess come out of the lift and drop off their keys. The doorman calls them a taxi. Ward gives the address of a restaurant in the Madeleine area.

Lapointe had been watching as Maigret continued with his reading.

'I went to the restaurant,' he said. 'Nothing to report. They often had dinner there and were always given the same table. Three or four people came and shook the colonel's hand. The couple didn't seem to be arguing. While the countess was eating her dessert, the colonel, who never had dessert, lit a cigar and looked through the evening papers.'

About 11.30. The couple arrive at the Monseigneur.

'They were regulars there, too,' Lapointe said, 'and there was even a tune that the gypsy orchestra automatically played as soon as the countess appeared. They ordered champagne and whisky. The colonel never danced.'

Maigret imagined the colonel, first at the restaurant, where he took advantage of the fact that he didn't require a dessert to read his newspaper, then on the red velvet banquette at the Monseigneur. He didn't dance, didn't flirt either, because he had known his companion for a long time. The musicians came and played at his table.

'*They were regulars there, too,*' Lapointe had said.

Three evenings, four evenings a week? And elsewhere, in London, Cannes, Rome, Lausanne, they frequented almost identical nightclubs, where the same tune was probably played when the countess came in and the colonel never danced.

He had a grown-up son of sixteen, in Cambridge, whom he phoned for a few minutes every three days, and a daughter in Switzerland he probably also phoned.

He'd had three wives: the first, who had remarried, led an existence similar to his, then Alice Perrin, who divided her time between London and Paris, and finally Muriel Halligan, a member of the single women's club.

In the streets, people were leaving work and hurrying towards the Métro entrances and the bus stops.

'We're here, chief.'

'I know.'

The courtyard of Quai des Orfèvres, which was growing dark, the staircase, as grey as ever, even though the lights were on.

He didn't go to see Lucas right away, but went into his own office, switched on the light and sat down in his normal seat, with Lapointe's memo in front of him.

00.15. Ward is called to the telephone. Unable to find out where the call came from.

Almost without thinking, Maigret reached out his hand to the telephone.

'Get me my apartment . . . Hello, is that you? . . . I'm back . . . Yes, I'm in my office . . . I don't know yet . . . Everything's fine . . . No, no, not at all. Why should I be sad?'

Why on earth had his wife asked him that question? He'd only wanted to get back in touch with her, that was all.

About 00.30. Marco Palmieri and Anna de Groot arrive at the Monseigneur.

(*Note*: Anna de Groot left the George-V at 7 p.m. She was alone. She met Marco at Fouquet's, where they had a quick dinner before going to the theatre. Neither was in evening dress. They are known at both Fouquet's and the Monseigneur, and their relationship is considered more or less official.)

Maigret was becoming aware of the amount of coming and going this report represented, the patience that Lapointe had shown to obtain information that was apparently of such little importance.

00.55. The barman of the George-V announces to his five or six remaining customers that he is about to close. John T. Arnold orders a Havana cigar and takes the three men he has been playing cards with out into the lobby.

(*Note*: I've been unable to establish with any certainty if Arnold left the bar during the evening. The barman couldn't say for sure. All the tables, as well as all the stools, were occupied up until ten in the evening. It was then that he noticed Arnold, in the left corner, near the window, in the company of three Americans who had recently arrived, including a film producer and an actor's agent. They were playing poker. Also unable to find out if Arnold already knew them or if he made their acquaintance that evening in the bar. They used chips, but when they finished the barman saw dollars change hands. He thinks they were playing for high stakes. He doesn't know who won.)

1.10. The waiter is called to the small Empire drawing room at the far end of the lobby and is asked if it is still possible to get a drink. He says yes, and they ask him for a bottle of whisky, some soda and four glasses. The four customers from the bar have chosen this place to continue their game.

1.55. Entering the Empire drawing room, the waiter sees that they have gone. The bottle is almost empty, the chips on the table, cigar butts in the ashtray.

(Questioned the night porter about this. The producer's name is Mark P. Jones and he is in France with a famous American comedian who is due to shoot a film or parts of a film in the south. Art Levinson is the star's agent. The third player is unknown to the porter. He has seen him several times in the lobby, but he isn't a guest of the hotel. He thinks he saw him leave that night at about two in the morning. I asked him if Arnold was with him. He can't say yes or no. He was on the telephone, as a guest on the fifth floor was complaining of the racket her neighbours were making. He went up himself and diplomatically asked the couple in question to keep the noise down.)

Maigret sat back in his chair and slowly filled his pipe, looking out at the grey evening beyond the windows.

About 2.05. The colonel and the countess leave the Monseigneur, take a taxi that is parked outside the nightclub and are driven to the George-V. I easily traced the taxi. The couple didn't utter a word during the ride.

2.15. They arrive at the George-V and get their keys from the porter. The colonel asks if there are any messages for him. There are none. Conversation while waiting for the lift, which takes a while to come down. They don't seem to be quarrelling.

2.18. The floor waiter is called to Suite 332. The colonel in an armchair, looking tired, as usual at that hour. The countess facing him, busy taking off her shoes and rubbing her feet. She orders a bottle of champagne and a bottle of whisky.

About 3.00. Anna de Groot returns, accompanied by Count Marco Palmieri. Cheerful and affectionate, but discreet. She is a little more animated than he is, probably because of the champagne. They talk to each other in English, even though both of them speak fluent French, the Dutch woman with a pronounced accent. The lift. A few moments later, they ring and ask for mineral water.

3.35. There is a call from 332. The countess tells the switchboard operator that she thinks she is dying and asks for a doctor. The switchboard operator first calls the nurse, then phones Dr Frère.

Maigret skimmed quickly through the rest, stood up, opened the door to the inspectors' room and found Lucas sitting by the light of his green-shaded lamp, talking on the telephone.

'I don't understand,' Lucas was crying in an exasperated tone. 'I keep telling you I don't understand a word you're saying. I don't even know what language you're speaking . . . No, I don't have an interpreter handy.'

He hung up and mopped his forehead.

'If I understood correctly, that was a call from

Copenhagen. I don't know if they were talking German or Danish . . . It hasn't stopped since this morning. Everyone wants to know everything.'

He stood up, embarrassed.

'I'm sorry, I haven't even asked you if you had a good trip . . . By the way, I had a call for you from Lausanne to say that the countess is taking the night train and will get to Paris at seven in the morning.'

'Did she call you herself?'

'No. The person you had lunch with.'

It was kind of him, and Maigret appreciated the tactful way he had dealt with it. A discreet helping hand . . . The director of the Lausanne Sûreté hadn't left his name, and Maigret, who hadn't kept his card, had already forgotten it.

'What has Arnold been doing today?' Maigret asked.

'First thing this morning, he went to a hotel on Faubourg Saint-Honoré, the Bristol, where Philps, the English solicitor, is staying.'

The Englishman hadn't gone to the George-V, too international to his taste, or the Scribe, too French, but had chosen to stay opposite the British Embassy, as if determined not to feel too far from his own country.

'They spent an hour conferring, then went together to an American bank on Avenue de l'Opéra, then to an English bank on Place Vendôme. In both, they were immediately seen by the manager. They were there for quite a long time. At exactly midday, they parted on Place Vendôme, and the solicitor took a taxi back to his hotel, where he had lunch alone.'

'And Arnold?'

'He crossed the Tuileries on foot, without hurrying, like a man who has all the time in the world, sometimes looking at his watch to make sure. He even browsed for a while among the second-hand booksellers by the Seine, leafing through old books and looking at prints, then, at a quarter to one, presented himself at the Hôtel des Grands-Augustins. He waited in the bar, drinking a Martini and glancing at the papers. Ward's third wife soon joined him.'

'Muriel Halligan?'

'Yes. She usually stays at that hotel. Apparently she'd arrived at Orly at about eleven thirty. When she got to the hotel, she took a bath and rested for half an hour before going to the bar.'

'Did she phone?'

'No.'

Which meant that she must have arranged to meet Arnold from Lausanne before leaving.

'Did they have lunch together?'

'Yes, in a little restaurant in Rue Jacob that looks like a bistro, but is very expensive. Torrence, who went in after them, says the food is wonderful and the bill is pretty steep . . . They chatted away happily, like old friends, but not loudly enough for Torrence to catch anything. Then Arnold walked her back to her hotel and took a taxi to join Monsieur Philps at the Bristol. The telephone didn't stop ringing, with calls from London, Cambridge, Amsterdam and Lausanne. Several people went up to the suite, including a Parisian notary named Monsieur Demonteau, who stayed longer than the others. There's a group of reporters in the lobby, waiting to find out when the funeral will be, and if it'll be in Paris, London or Lausanne. Supposedly, Ward was officially domiciled in Lausanne. They're also keen to know about the will, but so far they haven't got hold of any information. But they have reported that Ward's two children are expected any time now . . . You look tired, chief.'

'No . . . I don't know . . .'

He was more sluggish than usual and would honestly have been hard put to say what he was thinking about. It was the same experience as after a sea voyage: he still had the movement of the plane in his body, and his head was buzzing with images. It had all been too quick. Too many people, too many things one after the other. Joseph Van Meulen, naked on his bed, in the hands of his masseur, then leaving him in the lobby of the Hôtel de Paris to go in his dinner suit to a gala at the Sporting Club . . . The little countess with her crumpled face, hollows at the sides of her nose, her hands shaking from the alcohol . . . Then the fair-haired director of the Lausanne Sûreté – what was his name? – serving him a very clear, very cool wine with a candid smile, tinged with a slight irony towards the people he was talking about . . . The single women's club . . .

Now, in addition, he had the four men playing poker in the bar, then in the Empire drawing room . . .

And Monsieur Philps, in his English hotel opposite the British Embassy, the bank managers putting themselves out . . . Meetings, telephone calls, Monsieur Demonteau the notary, the reporters in the lobby of the Bristol and at the door of the George-V even though there was no longer anything to be seen there . . .

A young man in Cambridge, doubtless on his way to being a billionaire himself one day, who had suddenly learned that his father, who had phoned him the previous evening from a hotel on the continent, was dead . . .

And a girl of fourteen, envied perhaps by her schoolmates because she was packing her bags to go to her father's funeral . . .

By this hour, the little countess must be drunk, but she would still take the night train. All she had to do, whenever she felt faint, was have another drink to pick herself up. Until she fell.

'You look as if you have an idea, chief.'

'Me?'

He shrugged, as if freeing himself from a spell. And it was his turn to ask a question:

'Are you very tired?'

'Not too tired.'

'In that case, let's go and have a nice quiet dinner together at the Brasserie Dauphine.'

There, they wouldn't find the same clientele as at the George-V, or on the planes, or in Monte Carlo or Lausanne. A heavy kitchen smell, the same you found in country inns. The mother at her oven, the father behind the tin counter, the daughter helping the waiter to serve.

'And then?'

'Then I want to start all over again, as if I knew nothing, as if I didn't know these people.'

'Do you want me to go with you?'

'There's no need. To do what I have to do, I'd rather be alone.'

Lucas knew what that meant. Maigret was going to prowl Avenue George-V, sullenly puffing at his pipe, glancing right and left, sitting down here and there and getting up again almost immediately as if he didn't know what to do with his big body.

Nobody, not even he himself, could say how long it would last, but while it did, there was nothing pleasant about it.

Once, someone who had seen him like that had remarked, not very respectfully:

'He looks like a big, sick animal!'

7.

In which not only does Maigret feel unwanted, but he is regarded with suspicion

He took the Métro because he had plenty of time and he wasn't planning to move about a lot tonight. It was almost as if he had deliberately eaten too much, in order to feel even heavier. When he had left Lucas on Place Dauphine, the sergeant had hesitated then had opened his mouth to say something, and Maigret had looked at him expectantly.

'No, nothing,' Lucas had decided.

'Go on, say it.'

'I almost asked you if it was worth my going to bed.'

Because when the chief was in that mood, it generally meant that it wouldn't be long before the last act was played out within the four walls of his office.

As if by chance, that almost always happened at night, with the rest of the building in darkness, and sometimes several of them took turns with the person, man or woman, who came in to headquarters as a simple suspect and left, after a shorter or longer time, with handcuffs on their wrists.

Maigret understood what was in Lucas' mind. Without

being superstitious, he didn't like to anticipate events, and at that moment he had no confidence in himself.

'Go to bed.'

He didn't feel hot. He had left home on the morning of the previous day, sure that he would be returning to Boulevard Richard-Lenoir at midday for lunch. Was it just the previous day? It seemed to him that it was much longer since all this had begun.

He came out of the Métro on to the Champs-Élysées. The avenue was brightly lit, and the late-autumn weather was mild enough for there still to be crowds on the café terraces. His hands in his jacket pockets, he turned on to Avenue George-V, where, outside the hotel, a uniformed giant threw him a surprised glance on seeing him pushing the revolving door.

It was the night doorman. The previous day, Maigret had seen the daytime staff. The doorman was clearly wondering what this grumpy-looking man, his suit creased from travelling, who wasn't a guest of the hotel, was doing here.

There was the same curiosity, the same surprise on the part of the bellboy on duty on the other side of the revolving door and he was on the point of asking him what he wanted.

Some twenty people were scattered around the lobby, most in dinner jackets or evening dress, there were minks and diamonds, and as you walked past them you smelled first one perfume, then another.

As the bellboy wouldn't take his eyes off him, ready to follow and tackle him if he ventured too far, Maigret preferred to go straight to the desk, where the reception-ists in their yellow morning coats were unfamiliar.

'Is Monsieur Gilles in his office?'

'He's gone home. What is it you want?'

He had often noticed, in hotels, that the night staff were less friendly than the day staff. You almost always got the impression that they were second-class staff who resented the whole world for obliging them to live against the grain, to work while everybody else is asleep.

'Detective Chief Inspector Maigret,' he said.

'Do you want to go upstairs?'

'I probably will. I just want to warn you that I'm plan-ning to walk about the hotel for a while. Don't worry, I'll be as discreet as possible.'

'The keys to 332 are no longer with the porter. I have them here. The suites have been left as they were, at the request of the examining magistrate.'

'I know.'

He stuffed the keys in his pocket and, embarrassed by his hat, looked for somewhere to put it, finally placed it on an armchair and sat down in another one, just like anybody else waiting for somebody in the lobby.

From there, he saw the receptionist pick up the tele-phone and guessed that it was to inform the manager of his visit. A few moments later, he was proved right when the receptionist came up to him.

'I just spoke to Monsieur Gilles on the phone. I'm giving instructions to the staff to let you move around as you wish. Monsieur Gilles does ask, though, that—'

'I know, I know! Does Monsieur Gilles live in the hotel?'

'No. He has a villa in Sèvres.'

In order to question the night porter, Lapointe had had to go to Joinville. The barman, Maigret knew, lived even further from Paris, in the Chevreuse Valley, where he cultivated a rather large vegetable garden and raised chickens and ducks.

Wasn't it paradoxical? The guests paid astronomical sums to sleep as close as possible to the Champs-Élysées, while the staff, at least those who could afford that luxury, escaped to the country as soon as their work was over.

The groups standing, especially the groups in evening dress, were people who hadn't yet dined and were waiting until everyone had arrived to go to Maxim's, the Tour d'Argent or some other high-class restaurant. There were some in the bar, too, having a last cocktail before starting on what for them was the most important part of the day: dinner and the period after dinner.

Things must have happened the same way the day before yesterday, with an identical cast of extras. The florist in her booth was preparing buttonholes. The theatre person was handing over tickets to latecomers. The porter was giving directions to those who didn't yet know where to go.

Maigret had deliberately drunk a calvados after his dinner, just to be contradictory, because he was about to plunge back into a world in which people rarely drank calvados, let alone marc, but rather, whisky, champagne and Napoleon brandy.

A group of South Americans cheered a young woman in a straw-coloured mink coat who came rushing out of one of the lifts, making an entrance worthy of a film star.

Was she pretty? The little countess was also said to be amazing, and Maigret had seen her at close quarters, without make-up, and had even caught her drinking whisky straight from the bottle like a drunk swigging red wine on the river bank.

Why, in the last few moments, had he had the feeling he was on a ship? The atmosphere of the lobby reminded him of his trip to the United States, where an American billionaire – yet another billionaire! – had begged him to come and sort out a case. He remembered what he had been told by the purser one night when they had been the last people in the lounge, after the rather childish games held there were over.

'Did you know, inspector, that in first class there are three people to serve one passenger?'

It was true: every twenty metres, on the decks, in the lounges, on the gangways, you ran into a member of staff, in a white jacket or a uniform, ready to perform a service for you.

It was the same here. In the rooms, there were three bells, one to summon the head waiter, one the chambermaid, one the valet, and beside each bell — couldn't all the guests read? – the silhouette of the respective employee.

Outside the door, in the yellowish light of the pavement, two or three doormen, as well as luggage porters in their green aprons, stood to attention, as if at the entrance to a barracks, and in every corner, other men in uniform waited, standing very upright, their eyes staring into space.

'Believe it or not,' the purser had continued, 'the hardest thing on a ship isn't working the engines, performing a manoeuvre, sailing in rough weather, or getting to New York or Le Havre on time. Nor is it feeding a population equal to that of a sub-prefecture, or keeping the cabins, the lounges and the dining rooms clean. What gives us the most trouble is . . .'

He had paused.

'. . . *keeping the passengers entertained*. They have to be occupied from the moment they get up to the moment they go to bed, and some don't go to bed until dawn.'

That was why, as soon as breakfast was over, broth was served on deck. Then the games started, and the cocktails, followed by the caviar, the foie gras, the duckling with orange and the flambé omelettes . . .

'Most of them are people who've seen everything, who've amused themselves in every imaginable way, and yet at all costs we have to . . .'

To stop himself dozing off, Maigret stood up and went in search of the Empire drawing room, which he finally discovered, dimly lit and solemn at this hour, empty apart from a white-haired old gentleman in a dinner jacket asleep in an armchair, his mouth open, an extinguished cigar between his fingers. A little further on was the dining room, and the head waiter standing guard at the door looked him up and down. He didn't offer him a table. Had he realized that he wasn't a true guest?

In spite of his reproving look, Maigret glanced into the

room, where, beneath the chandeliers, some ten tables were occupied.

An idea, not a very original one to be sure, was forming in his mind. He passed a lift beside which stood a fair-haired young man in olive livery. It wasn't the lift he had taken with the manager on the morning of the previous day. And elsewhere, he discovered a third one.

Everyone was watching him. The head receptionist hadn't had time to alert all the staff. He had probably only informed the heads of departments of Maigret's presence.

Nobody asked him what he wanted, what he was looking for, where he was going, but he only moved away from one set of suspicious eyes to enter another area just as jealously guarded.

His little idea . . . It wasn't very specific yet, and yet he had the impression he had made an important discovery. What it amounted to was this: wouldn't these people – and in this he included the guests of the George-V, those in Monte Carlo and Lausanne, the Wards, the Van Meulens, the Countess Palmieris, all those who led this kind of existence – wouldn't these people feel lost, helpless, naked somehow, as powerless, clumsy and fragile as babies, if suddenly they were plunged into everyday life?

Would they be able to elbow their way into a Métro carriage, consult the railway timetable, buy their own tickets, carry their own suitcases?

Here, from the moment they left their suites to the moment they settled into an identical suite in New York, London or Lausanne, they didn't have to worry about their luggage, which passed from hand to hand, almost as if without their knowledge, and they found their things already set out for them. They themselves passed from hand to hand . . .

What had Van Meulen said about *sufficient motive*? Someone who has sufficient motive to commit murder . . .

Maigret was beginning to realize that it wasn't even about a larger or smaller sum of money. He was even starting to understand those American divorcees who demanded to live the rest of their lives in the manner to which their ex-husbands had accustomed them.

He couldn't see the little countess going into a bistro, ordering a milky coffee, handling an automatic telephone.

That was the minor aspect of the question, of course. But aren't the minor aspects often the most important? In an apartment, would Countess Palmieri be capable of adjusting the central heating, lighting the gas stove in the kitchen, boiling herself eggs?

His thought was more complicated than that, so complicated that it lacked clarity.

How many of such people were there in the world, going from one place to another, sure of finding everywhere the same atmosphere, the same diligent attention, the same people, so to speak, who took care of all the little details of existence for them?

A few thousand, probably. The purser of the *Liberté* had also said to him:

'You can't invent anything new to distract them, because they cling to their habits.'

Just as they clung to the same decor. An identical decor,

give or take a few details. Was it a way of reassuring themselves, of giving themselves the illusion that they were at home? Even the position of the mirrors in the bedrooms, or of the tie rack, was the same everywhere.

'It's pointless to take up our profession if you don't have a good memory for names and faces.'

It wasn't the ship's purser who had said that, but the porter in a hotel on the Champs-Élysées where Maigret had conducted an investigation twenty years earlier.

'The guests expect to be recognized, even if they've only been here once before.'

That, too, probably reassured them. Little by little, Maigret was feeling less harsh towards them. It was as if they were afraid of something, afraid of themselves, of reality, of solitude. They moved around in circles in a small number of places, where they were sure of receiving the same care, the same consideration, eating the same dishes, drinking the same champagne or the same whisky.

It might not have amused them, but once they got into the habit, *they would have been incapable of living any other way.*

Was that *sufficient motive*? Maigret was starting to think it was, and as a result, Colonel Ward's death took on a new meaning.

Someone in his entourage had been – or had felt – threatened with having suddenly to live like everybody else, and had been unable to face it.

But that meant that Ward's death would have to allow this someone to continue to lead the existence he or she could not bear giving up.

Nothing was known of the will. Maigret still didn't know with which notary or solicitor it was. John T. Arnold implied that there were several wills, all in different hands.

Wasn't Maigret wasting his time prowling like this in the corridors of the George-V? Wouldn't the most sensible thing be to go home to bed and wait?

He went into the bar. The night barman didn't know him either, but one of the waiters recognized him from his photographs and whispered something to his boss, who frowned. He wasn't flattered to be serving Detective Chief Inspector Maigret – on the contrary, it seemed to make him nervous.

There were a lot of people, a lot of cigar and cigarette smoke, and only one pipe apart from Maigret's.

'What can I get you?'

'Do you have calvados?'

He couldn't see any on the shelf, where all the brands of whisky were lined up. The barman nevertheless dug out a bottle and grabbed a huge balloon-shaped tasting glass, as if that were the only kind of glass available here for spirits.

Most people were speaking English. Maigret recognized a woman, a mink stole casually thrown over her shoulders, who'd had dealings at Quai des Orfèvres in the days when she had worked for a minor Corsican pimp in Montmartre.

That was two years earlier. She hadn't wasted any time: she was wearing a diamond ring on her finger and a diamond bracelet around her wrist. She nevertheless condescended to recognize Maigret and give him a discreet wink.

Three men were sitting around a table at the far end, on the left, near the silk-curtained window, and Maigret asked on the off chance:

'Isn't that Mark Jones, the producer?'

'The fat little man, yes.'

'Which one is Art Levinson?'

'The one with very brown hair and tortoiseshell glasses.'

'And the third man?'

'I've seen him several times, but I don't know him.'

The barman was answering reluctantly, as if loath to betray his customers.

'How much do I owe you?'

'No, it's all right.'

'I insist on paying.'

'Oh, well, it's up to you.'

He didn't take the lift, but climbed slowly to the third floor, thinking as he did so that few of the guests probably trod the red carpet on the stairs. He met a woman in black, a notebook in her hand, a pencil behind her ear, who was something in the hotel hierarchy. He assumed, because she had a bunch of keys at her belt, that it was she who supervised the chambermaids on some of the floors and made sure the sheets and towels were distributed.

She turned to look at him, seemed to hesitate, and probably went straight to inform the management of the presence of a curious individual behind the scenes at the George-V.

Because, unwittingly, he found himself suddenly behind

the scenes, in a kind of backstage area. He had opened the door through which the woman had come and discovered another staircase, this one narrower and uncarpeted. The walls were no longer so white. A half-open door revealed a cubbyhole cluttered with brooms and a big pile of dirty linen in the middle.

There was nobody about. Nobody on the next floor either, in another room, this one more spacious, furnished with a table and chairs in white wood. There was a tray on the table, with plates, the bones of some cutlets, sauce and a few congealed fried potatoes.

Above the door, he discovered a set of bells, three bulbs of different colours.

In an hour, he saw a lot of things and came across a number of people: waiters, chambermaids, a valet polishing shoes. Most looked at him in surprise, and followed him suspiciously with their eyes. But with one exception, nobody spoke to him.

Perhaps they assumed that if he was here, he had the right to be here. Or did they hurry to phone the management when his back was turned?

He came across a worker in overalls carrying plumbers' tools, which suggested there were problems with the pipes somewhere in the hotel. The man, a cigarette stuck to his lips, looked him up and down and asked:

'Looking for something?'

'No. Thank you.'

The man walked away with a shrug of his shoulders, turned and finally disappeared behind a door.

Uninterested in the two suites he already knew, Maigret

climbed higher than the third floor, familiarizing himself with the place. He had learned to recognize the doors that separated the corridors with their spotless walls and thick carpeting from the less luxurious backstage areas with their narrow staircases.

Moving from one side to the other, spotting here a service lift, there a waiter asleep on a chair, or two chambermaids busy telling each other their illnesses, he finally came out on to the roof, surprised to suddenly see the stars above him and the colourful reflected glow of the lights of the Champs-Élysées in the sky.

He stayed there for a while, emptying his pipe, walking around the roof, leaning from time to time over the handrail, watching as the cars glided noiselessly along the avenue, stopped outside the hotel and left again filled with richly dressed women and gentlemen in black and white.

Opposite, Rue François-Ier was brightly lit, and the English pharmacy on the corner of the street and Avenue George-V was still open. Was it the duty pharmacy? Was it open every evening? Given the pampered clientele of the George-V and its neighbouring hotel, the Prince de Galles, who lived life the wrong way round, coming alive at night rather than during the day, it probably did excellent business.

On the left, the quieter Rue Christophe-Colomb was lit only by the red neon sign of a restaurant or nightclub, and large, shiny cars dozed alongside both kerbs.

Behind, in Rue Magellan, was a bar, the kind of drivers' bistro you saw in wealthy neighbourhoods. A man in a white jacket crossed the street and went in, doubtless a waiter.

Maigret was thinking in slow motion, and it took him a while to retrace the route that had led him to the roof. Later, losing his way, he came across the head waiter eating scraps from a tray.

By the time he got back to the hotel bar, it was eleven o'clock, and there were fewer customers. The three Americans he had seen earlier were still in their places and along with a fourth man, also an American, very tall and thin, were playing poker.

The fourth man's high-heeled shoes intrigued Maigret for a moment until he realized that in fact they were cowboy boots, with ankles of multi-coloured leather hidden by his trousers. A man from Texas or Arizona. He was more demonstrative than the others, spoke in a loud voice, and you fully expected him to draw a gun from his belt.

Maigret finally sat down on a stool and the barman asked him:

'The same?'

He nodded and asked in his turn:

'Do you know him?'

'I don't know his name, but he owns an oil well. Apparently, the pumps work by themselves. The man doesn't have to do a thing and still makes a million a day.'

'Was he here the night before last?'

'No. He arrived this morning. He's leaving again tomorrow for Cairo and Arabia, where he has interests.'

'Were the other three here?'

'Yes.'

'With Arnold?'

'Wait . . . The night before last . . . Yes. One of your inspectors already asked me that.'

'I know. Who's the third man, the fair-haired one?'

'I don't know his name. He isn't staying at this hotel. I think he's at the Crillon and I'm told he owns a chain of restaurants.'

'Does he speak French?'

'None of them do, apart from Monsieur Levinson, who lived in Paris when he wasn't yet a film star's agent.'

'Do you know what he did before?'

The barman shrugged.

'Could you go and ask the man who's staying at the Crillon a question from me?'

The barman grimaced but didn't dare say no.

'What question?' he asked unenthusiastically.

'I'd like to know where he and Monsieur Arnold parted when he left here the night before last.'

The barman walked over to the poker players' table, preparing his smile as he did so. He leaned over the third man, who looked curiously in Maigret's direction, after which the other three did the same, having just learned who he was. The answer was longer than might have been expected.

At last, the barman returned, while the game resumed in the corner.

'He asked me why you needed to know that. He pointed out that this isn't the way things are done in his country. He didn't remember immediately. He drank a lot the night before last. It'll be the same tonight by the time we close. They continued their game in the Empire drawing room.'

'That, I know.'

'He lost ten thousand dollars, but he's making up for it tonight.'

'Did Arnold win?'

'I didn't ask. He thinks he remembers saying goodbye to him at the door of the Empire drawing room. He told me he'd assumed Arnold was staying at the George-V, but he's only known him for a few days.'

Maigret didn't react. He spent a good quarter of an hour over his drink, vaguely watching the poker players. The girl he had recognized was no longer there, but there was another one, on her own, who so far could only afford fake diamonds and seemed as interested in the game as he was.

Maigret pointed her out to the barman.

'I didn't think you allowed these women . . .'

'In principle. We make an exception for two or three we know who behave themselves. It's almost a necessity. Otherwise, the guests will pick up God knows what outside. You wouldn't imagine the creatures they sometimes bring back.'

For a moment, Maigret thought . . . No! First of all, the colonel hadn't been robbed. Plus, it would have been out of character . . .

'Are you leaving?'

'I may be back later.'

He intended to wait until three in the morning, which meant he still had time to kill. Not sure where to put himself, he prowled again, sometimes on the guest side, sometimes on the staff side. There was less coming and going as the night wore on. He saw two or three couples come back from the theatre, heard bells ring, passed a waiter with bottles of beer on a tray, and another on his way to serve a complete meal.

At one point, turning a corner in a corridor, he almost crashed into the head receptionist.

'Do you need me for anything, inspector?'

'No, thanks.'

The man was pretending to be there to help him, but Maigret was convinced he had come to check up on what he was doing.

'Most guests don't get back until three in the morning.'

'I know. Thank you.'

'If you need anything . . .'

'I'll ask you.'

The man moved away, then retraced his steps.

'I did give you the keys, didn't I?'

Maigret's presence in the hotel clearly made him uncomfortable. But the inspector continued with his wandering. He found himself in the basement area, as vast as the crypt of a cathedral, and glimpsed men in blue overalls working in a boiler room that could have been that of a ship.

Here, too, people turned to look at him. An employee in a glass cage was checking off the bottles coming from the wine cellar. In the kitchens, women were busy washing down the tiled floor.

Another staircase, lit by a lamp enclosed in wire

netting, a swing door, another glass cage, this one with nobody in it. The air was cooler here, and when Maigret opened a second door he was surprised to find himself out in the street. On the opposite pavement, a man in shirt-sleeves was lowering the shutter of the small bar he had seen from the roof.

He was in Rue Magellan. The Champs-Élysées was to his right, at the end of Rue Bassano. In the next doorway, a couple stood clasped in each other's arms. Could the man be the hotel employee who should have been in the glass cage?

Was this exit guarded day and night? Did the staff have to clock in and out? Hadn't Maigret seen a waiter in a white jacket earlier, crossing the street and going into the bar opposite?

He registered all these details mechanically. By the time he got back to the hotel bar, the lights were off, the poker players were no longer there, and the waiters were busy clearing the tables.

He didn't find his four Americans in the Empire drawing room either. It was empty and looked like a silent chapel.

When he saw the barman again, the man was in a lounge suit, and Maigret almost didn't recognize him.

'Have the poker players gone?'

'I think they went up to Mark Jones's suite. They'll probably play all night. Are you staying? . . . Goodnight, then.'

It was still only 1.15 when Maigret walked into the late David Ward's suite. Everything was still in its place, including the scattered clothes and the water in the bath.

He didn't conduct a search, merely settled in an arm-chair, lit a pipe and stayed there, dozing.

Perhaps he had been wrong to rush to Orly, to Nice, to Monte Carlo, to Lausanne. Talking of which, the little countess must be asleep in her sleeper car by now. Was she going to stay at the George-V as usual? Was she still hoping that Marco would take her back?

She was nothing now, neither Ward's wife, nor his widow, nor Marco's wife. She had admitted that she had no money. How long would she be able to live off her furs and jewellery?

Had the colonel foreseen that he might die before his divorce from Muriel Halligan had become final and he'd married the countess?

It was unlikely.

She wouldn't even have the means to join the single women's club in Lausanne, those women who, when they ate out, ordered dishes without salt or butter, but still drank four or five cocktails before every meal.

Didn't she answer the criteria listed by Van Meulen?

He wasn't trying to reach a conclusion, to solve a problem. He wasn't thinking, he was letting his mind roam at will.

Everything might depend on a little experiment. And even then, the experiment wouldn't necessarily be con-clusive. It was a good thing the reporters who praised his methods didn't know how he sometimes operated: his reputation would be bound to suffer.

Twice, he almost fell asleep, waking with a start just in time to look at his watch. The second time, it was 2.30, and to stay awake he decided to change scenery. He went to suite 332, where all that had been done, as a precaution, was to take away the countess's jewels and store them in the hotel's safe.

Nobody, it seemed, had touched the bottle of whisky and, after about ten minutes, Maigret went to the bathroom, rinsed a glass and poured himself a drink.

At last, at three o'clock, he went back through the door into the backstage area, passing a fairly tipsy couple as he did so. The woman was singing and carrying on her arm, like a baby, a huge white teddy bear she must have been sold in a nightclub.

He ran into just one waiter, a grim-faced man who looked as if he should have retired. Finding his bearings, he went downstairs, too far down at first, then back up to the first level of the basement, at last discovering the glass cage, in which there was still nobody, then the brisk air of Rue Magellan.

The bar opposite had long since closed. He had seen the shutter being lowered. The red neon light in the next street was off, and, although the cars were still there, he didn't see anyone on the pavement. It wasn't until he got to Rue Bassano that he saw a pedestrian, who sped away as if afraid of him.

Fouquet's, on the corner of the Champs-Élysées, was also closed, as was the brasserie opposite. A girl standing against the wall of the travel agency said something to him in a low voice that he didn't understand.

On the other side of the avenue, where only a few cars were passing, two large windows were still alight, not far from the Lido.

Maigret hesitated at the kerb. He must have looked like a sleepwalker, because he was trying to put himself in the skin of another person, a person who had killed a man a few minutes earlier by holding his head under water in his bath and had then followed the same route from suite 347 as he had.

An empty taxi was coming down the avenue and slowed as it passed him. Had the murderer hailed a taxi? Or had he told himself that it was dangerous, that the police almost always tracked down the driver who took such and such a route?

He let it pass and almost continued along the same side of the street in the direction of the Concorde.

Then he looked again at the lighted bar on the other side of the street, with its long brass counter. From a distance, he saw the waiter serving beer, the cashier and four or five motionless customers, two of them women.

He crossed, hesitated again and at last went in.

The two women looked at him, started to smile, then, even though they didn't recognize him, seemed to realize that he wasn't a likely client.

Had something similar happened the night before last? The man behind the counter was also looking at him questioningly, waiting for his order.

Maigret had a bad taste in his mouth from the whisky. His gaze fell on the beer pump.

'I'll have a beer.'

Outside, two or three women emerged from the darkness and peered at him through the window.

One of them ventured into the bar then went straight

back out, where she presumably told the others that he was a dead loss.

'Are you open all night?'

'Yes, all night.'

'Are there any other bars open between here and the Madeleine?'

'Only strip clubs.'

'Were you here two nights ago at the same time?'

'I'm here every night except Monday.'

'What about you?' he asked the cashier, who had a blue woollen shawl over her shoulders.

'My day off is Wednesday.'

The night before last had been a Tuesday. So they had both been here.

He pointed to the two girls and said in a low voice:

'What about them?'

'Except when they take a client to Rue Washington or Rue de Berri . . .'

The waiter was frowning, wondering who this strange customer, whose face reminded him of something, could possibly be. It was one of the girls who recognized him in the end and moved her lips to warn the waiter.

She didn't think that Maigret could see her in the mirror, and kept saying the same word, moving her mouth like a fish. The waiter didn't understand, looked at her, then looked at the inspector and looked at her again questioningly.

In the end, Maigret had to interpret:

'Watch out, cops about!'

And as the waiter still didn't seem to know what was going on, he explained:

'She's telling you I'm a policeman.'
'And are you?'
'Yes.'
He must have been funny talking like this, because the girl, after a moment of embarrassment, couldn't stop herself from bursting into loud laughter.

8.

Those who saw and those who didn't, or the art of combining witnesses

'No chief, I don't mind at all. I was expecting it. I even told my wife when we went to bed.'

Lucas had woken up as soon as the telephone had rung, but probably didn't have a clock within sight, and might not even have switched the light on in his bedroom.

'What time is it?'

'Half past three. Do you have a paper and a pencil?'

'Hold on . . .'

Through the window of the phone booth, Maigret could see the lavatory attendant asleep on her chair, her knitting in her lap, and he knew that upstairs, at the counter, they were talking about him.

'Go ahead.'

'I don't have time to explain. Just follow my instructions to the letter.'

He gave them slowly, repeating each sentence so that there should be no mistake.

'I'll see you later.'

'Not too tired, chief?'

'No, not too tired.'

He hung up and called Lapointe, who took longer to wake up, perhaps because he was younger.

'Go and have a glass of cold water first. Then listen . . .'

He gave him specific instructions, too. He thought about calling Janvier, but Janvier lived in the suburbs and probably wouldn't find a taxi immediately.

He went back upstairs. The girl who had offered to go and wait for Olga at the door of the rooming house in Rue Washington and bring her back hadn't yet returned, and Maigret had a second glass of beer. It might be making him a little heavier, but for what he had to do, that was probably for the best.

'Do I really have to go, too?' the waiter asked. 'Won't the two girls be enough? Even if he doesn't remember Malou, because he didn't speak to her, I'm sure he won't have forgotten Olga, and we're getting her for you. Not only did he buy her a drink and chat to her, but from what I understood he clearly wanted her to go with him. With her red hair and those breasts of hers, Olga isn't easy to forget.'

'I insist I want you there.'

'I'm not saying this for me, but for my workmate. I'm going to have to drag him out of bed, and he won't like it.'

The girl who had gone returned with the famous Olga, a flaming redhead, who did indeed display a voluminous chest.

'This is him,' her friend said to her. 'Detective Chief Inspector Maigret. Don't be afraid.'

Olga was still a little suspicious. Maigret bought her a drink and gave her instructions, as he had the others.

Alone at last, he left the bar and walked unhurriedly down the Champs-Élysées, puffing at his pipe, his hands in his pockets.

He passed the doorman outside Claridge's and almost stopped and recruited him, too. The only reason he didn't was that a little further on he saw an old woman sitting on the ground, her back to the wall, in front of a basket of flowers.

'Were you here the night before last?'

She looked up at him suspiciously, and he had to negotiate with her. He eventually got what he wanted, went over his instructions two or three times and handed her some money.

He could walk a little faster now. His cast was all assembled. Lucas and Lapointe would do the rest. He almost took a taxi, but he would have got there too late.

He reached Avenue Matignon, hesitated, then told himself that the man, accustomed to this route, must have taken a short cut via Faubourg Saint-Honoré. He passed the British Embassy and the hotel where Monsieur Philps was resting from the previous days' comings and goings.

The Madeleine, Boulevard des Capucines . . . Another man in uniform, at the door of the Scribe, a revolving door, a lobby less well lit than that of the George-V, rather more old-fashioned decor . . .

He showed his badge to the receptionist.

'Is Monsieur John T. Arnold in?'

A glance at the key rack. A nod.

'Has he been in bed long?'

'He got back about ten thirty.'

'Does he often do that?'

'Not usually, but with all that's happening, he had a very busy day.'

'What time did you see him come in last night?'

'Just after midnight.'

'And the night before last?'

'Much later.'

'After three?'

'It's possible. But as I'm sure you know, we're not allowed to provide information on the comings and goings of our guests.'

'Everyone's obliged to bear witness in a criminal case.'

'Then you must speak to the manager.'

'Was the manager here the night before last?'

'No, but I'll only talk with his authorization.'

He was stubborn, narrow-minded, disagreeable.

'Get me the manager on the phone.'

'I can only disturb him for a serious reason.'

'It's serious enough for me to put you in a police cell if you don't call him immediately.'

The man must finally have realized the gravity of the situation.

'In that case, I'll give you the information. It was after three, and even well after three thirty, because it was a little later that I had to go upstairs to stop the Italians making so much noise.'

Maigret gave him instructions, too, though he still had to speak to the manager of the hotel on the telephone.

'Now will you be kind enough to put me through to John T. Arnold? Just ring his suite. I'll talk to him.'

Holding the receiver, Maigret was quite nervous: this was a difficult, delicate game he was playing. He heard ringing in that suite he didn't know. Then the telephone was picked up at the other end.

'Monsieur Arnold?' he asked in a muted voice.

'Who is it?'

Half-asleep, Arnold had naturally spoken in his native language.

'I'm sorry to bother you, Monsieur Arnold. This is Detective Chief Inspector Maigret. I'm about to lay my hands on the person who murdered your friend Ward and I need your help.'

'Are you still in Lausanne?'

'No, in Paris.'

'When do you want to see me?'

'Right now.'

There was a silence, a hesitation.

'Where?'

'I'm downstairs in your hotel. I'd like to come up for a moment and talk to you.'

Another silence. Arnold had a perfect right to refuse this interview. Would he do so?

'Is it the countess you want to talk about?'

'About her, too, yes.'

'Did she come back with you? Is she with you now?'

'No, I'm alone.'

'All right. Come up.'

Maigret hung up, relieved.

'Which suite?' he asked the receptionist.

'551. The bellboy will take you.'

Corridors, numbered doors. They encountered a single waiter, who knocked at the door of 551 for them.

John T. Arnold's eyes were puffy, and he looked older than when Maigret had met him at the George-V. He was wearing a black dressing gown with a leaf pattern over silk pyjamas.

'Come in. Excuse the mess . . . What did the countess tell you? She's a hysteric, did you know that? And, when she's been drinking . . .'

'I know. I'm grateful to you for agreeing to see me. It's in everyone's interest – except for the murderer's, of course – for the case to be brought swiftly to a close, isn't it? I've heard that you and the English solicitor went to a great deal of trouble yesterday to sort out Ward's estate.'

'It's very complicated,' the pink little man sighed.

He had ordered tea from the waiter.

'Would you like some, too?'

'No, thank you.'

'Something else?'

'No. To tell the truth, Monsieur Arnold, it isn't here that I need you.'

Even though he pretended not to look at Arnold, he kept an eye on his reactions.

'At Quai des Orfèvres, my men have made a number of discoveries that I'd like to put to you.'

'What kind of discoveries?'

Maigret pretended not to have heard.

'I could obviously have waited until tomorrow morning

to summon you. But as you're the person who was closest to the colonel, and the most devoted, I didn't think you'd be too upset with me if I disturbed you in the middle of the night.'

He was as benign as he could possibly be, like a civil servant embarrassed at having to perform an unpleasant task.

'In cases like this, time is of the essence. You've spoken more than once of the importance of Ward's business affairs, the repercussions of his death in financial circles . . . If you don't mind, I'd like you to get dressed and come with me.'

'Where to?'

'My office.'

'Can't we talk here?'

'My office is the only place where I'll be able to show you the evidence and ask your advice on a number of matters.'

It took a little more time, but in the end, Arnold made up his mind to get dressed, moving from the sitting room to the bedroom, from the bedroom to the bathroom.

Not once did Maigret utter the name Muriel Halligan, but he spoke a lot about the countess, in a half-serious, half-amused tone. Arnold drank his scorching-hot tea. In spite of the hour, and the place they were going, he made himself as immaculate as usual.

'I don't suppose this'll take long, will it? I went to bed early because tomorrow I have an even busier day than today. You do know that Bobby, the colonel's son, has arrived with someone from his school? They're staying here.'

'Not at the George-V?'

'I thought it preferable, given what happened there.'

'You did the right thing.'

Maigret made no attempt to hurry him. Quite the contrary: he had to give Lucas and the others time to do all they had to do, to get everything ready.

'Your life is going to change a lot, isn't it? How long, by the way, were you with your friend Ward?'

'Nearly thirty years.'

'Going everywhere with him?'

'Everywhere.'

'And overnight . . . I wonder if it's because of him that you've never married.'

'What do you mean?'

'If you were married, you wouldn't have been as free to go with him. When it comes down to it, you sacrificed your personal life to him.'

Maigret would have preferred to go about it differently, to plant himself in front of this plump, well-groomed little man and say straight out:

'Just between ourselves, you killed Ward because . . .'

The unfortunate thing was that he didn't know why exactly, and Arnold would doubtless have shrugged off the accusation.

'Countess Palmieri will get into Gare de Lyon at seven. She's on the train right now.'

'What did she tell you?'

'That she went to the colonel's suite and found him dead.'

'Have you summoned her to Quai des Orfèvres?' He

frowned. 'You're not going to make me wait there until she arrives?'

'I don't think so.'

At last they both headed for the lift. Arnold automatically pressed the button.

'I forgot to take a coat.'

'I don't have one either. It isn't cold, and it'll only take a few minutes by taxi.'

Maigret didn't want to let him go back to his suite alone. As soon as they were in the cab, an inspector would conduct a thorough search of it.

They crossed the lobby quickly enough for Arnold not to notice that it wasn't the same man in reception. A taxi was waiting.

'Quai des Orfèvres!'

The boulevards were deserted. Couples here and there. A few taxis, mostly on their way to the railway stations. Maigret only had a few minutes left to play his disagreeable role and to wonder if he wasn't barking up the wrong tree.

The taxi didn't take them into the courtyard. The two men walked past the sentry and went in under the stone archway, where it was always colder than elsewhere.

'I'll show you the way.'

Maigret walked in front up the dimly lit main staircase. He held the glass door open for his companion. The vast corridor, on to which the doors of the various departments gave, was empty, with only two of the lights on.

'Just like a hotel at night!' Maigret thought, remembering all the corridors he had wandered down that night.

Out loud, he said:

'This way . . . Please come in.'

He didn't take Arnold to his own office, but to the inspectors' office. He himself stayed behind him, knowing the sight that awaited the Englishman on the other side of the door.

One step . . . Two steps . . . A pause . . . He was aware of a shiver running down Arnold's back, a movement to turn back that he was tempted to make but controlled.

'Go in.'

Closing the door behind them, he found that everything had been staged exactly as he had imagined. Lucas was sitting at his desk, apparently engrossed in writing a report. At the desk opposite, young Lapointe sat with a cigarette between his lips. Maigret noticed that of all of them he was the palest. Did he realize what a difficult, even dangerous, game Maigret was playing?

Along the walls, on chairs, bodies and faces as motionless as wax figures.

The extras hadn't been placed any old how, but in a specific order. First, in an overcoat open over his black trousers and white jacket, the night waiter who worked on the third floor of the George-V. Then a uniformed bellboy. Next, a little old man with bilious eyes, the man who ought by rights to be in the glass cage near the service entrance in Rue Magellan right now.

These three were the most ill at ease, and they avoided looking at Arnold, who couldn't have failed to recognize them, the first of them anyway, or the second because of his uniform.

The third could have been anybody. It didn't matter. Next came Olga, the redhead with the luxuriant breasts, who was chewing gum to overcome her irritation, and the friend who had gone to wait for her outside the rooming house in Rue Washington.

And finally, the waiter from the bar, also in an overcoat, with a check cap in his hand, the old flower-seller and the receptionist from the Scribe.

'I assume you know these people?' Maigret said. 'We'll go to my office and talk to them one by one. Do you have the written statements, Lucas?'

'Yes, chief.'

Maigret opened the communicating door.

'Please come in, Monsieur Arnold . . .'

Arnold stood there for a moment, rooted to the spot, his eyes fixed intensely on Maigret.

It was essential for Maigret to sustain that gaze, to keep his air of self-confidence.

He repeated:

'Please come in.'

He switched on the green-shaded lamp on his desk and pointed to an armchair facing his.

'You can smoke if you like.'

When he looked again at Arnold, he realized that the Englishman was still staring at him in genuine terror.

As naturally as possible, Maigret filled a pipe and said:

'And now, if you don't mind, we'll call in the witnesses one by one in order to establish your movements from the moment in Colonel Ward's bathroom when . . .'

As his hand moved ostentatiously to press the button,

he saw Arnold's prominent eyes mist over and his lower lip rise as if in a sob. But he didn't cry. Swallowing to relax the tension in his throat, he said in a voice that was painful to hear:

'There's no point.'

'Do you confess?'

A silence. A flicker of the eyelids.

And then something happened that was almost unique in Maigret's career. He had been so tense, so anxious, that there was a sudden collapse of his whole body, betraying the relief he felt.

Arnold, who hadn't taken his eyes off him, was stunned at first, then frowned and grew pale.

'You . . .'

The words emerged with difficulty.

'You didn't know, did you?'

At last, in a burst of realization:

'They never saw me, did they?'

'Not all of them,' Maigret admitted. 'I'm sorry, Monsieur Arnold, but it was best to have done with it, don't you think? It was the only way.'

Hadn't he saved him hours, perhaps whole days of interrogation?

'I assure you it's best for you, too.'

They were still waiting next door, all the witnesses, those who had really seen something and those who had seen nothing. By placing them in a row, in the order in which Arnold *might* have met them, Maigret had created the impression of a solid chain of testimonies.

In a way, the real ones made up for the fake ones.

'I assume I can let them go?'

Arnold did try to struggle a little.

'What is there to prove, right now, that—'

'Listen to me, Monsieur Arnold. Right now, as you say, I know. You might be able to retract your confession, and even claim it was extracted from you by violence.'

'I didn't say that.'

'But it's too late to turn the clock back. So far, I haven't seen fit to disturb a certain lady who's staying at a hotel on Quai des Grands-Augustins and with whom you had lunch yesterday. I can do that. She'll sit where you're sitting, and I'll ask her so many questions that she'll have to answer in the end.'

There was a heavy silence.

'You were planning to marry her, weren't you?'

No reply.

'How many days did you have before the divorce became final and she had to give up her claims to the estate?'

Without waiting, Maigret went and opened the window. The sky was starting to lighten, and tugboats could be heard calling to their barges upstream of the Ile Saint-Louis.

'Three days.'

Had he heard? As if everything was normal, Maigret opened the communicating door.

'You can go, everyone. I don't need you any more . . . Lucas!'

He had hesitated between Lucas and Lapointe. Seeing how disappointed the young man was, he added:

'You, too. Come in, both of you, and take his statement.'

He went back to the middle of his office, chose a fresh pipe, which he filled slowly, and looked around for his hat.

'Do you mind if I leave you, Monsieur Arnold?'

Arnold was slumped on his chair, suddenly very old. With every passing minute he was losing that . . . That what? Maigret would have found it hard to express what he was thinking. That indefinable sense of ease and brilliance, that self-assurance that distinguished the people who were part of a certain world, the people encountered in luxury hotels . . .

It was almost gone now, and he was just a man, an unhappy, shattered man who had played the game and lost.

'I'm going home to bed,' Maigret told his colleagues. 'If you need me . . .'

It was Lapointe who noticed that as Maigret passed John T. Arnold, he placed a hand on his shoulder for a moment, as if without thinking, and there was a troubled expression in the young inspector's eyes as he watched his chief walk to the door.

OTHER TITLES IN THE SERIES